8 March 1999

To Henry +
Oldest friend
friends — with love —

NOTHING GOLD CAN STAY

18 Stories of Israeli Experience

Jerome Mandel

Israel Federation of Writers Unions Tel Aviv

I am grateful to the editors for allowing me to reprint the following previously published stories. "Mothers" appeared in *War, Literature, and the Arts,* vol. 7.1 (1995). "Stone" appeared in *arc.* "The Orange" originally appeared in *arc* and in *Short Story International No. 88;* "Solange" originally appeared in *arc* and in *Short Story International No. 94* (where the title was "Brownout"). Both "Solange" and "The Orange" are reprinted by permission of International Cultural Exchange, Inc., Great Neck, New York. "Another Life" appeared in *The Missouri Review*, 19.3 (1996). "Third Time, Ice Cream," winner of the 1997 P.E.N.-UNESCO International Short-Story Prize, first appeared in *P.E.N.-International*, vol. 47, no. 2 (1997), and is reproduced by kind permission of International P.E.N. It also appeared in *P.E.N. Israel, arc,* and *Nativ* (in Hebrew). *Midstream* has accepted "The Present" for publication.

Portrait of Jerome Mandel © Michael Cohen.
Cover Photography © Michael Cohen.

Some of these stories were first read to an intelligent group of writers in Chayym Zeldis' writer's workshop in Ra'anana. My thanks to all of them for criticism in progress. I was fortunate, too, to spend six splendid weeks writing at The Hambidge Center in Rabun Gap, Georgia, among artists with different ideas about exactly what it was that we were doing and different ways of doing it.

ISBN 965-7030-03-X
Published by Israel Federation of Writers Unions
6 Kaplan St. Tel Aviv, Israel
TEL: 972-3-695-3737
FAX: 972-3-691-9681

Miriam

Nothing Gold Can Stay

Nature's first green is gold,
Her hardest hue to hold.
Her early leaf's a flower;
But only so an hour.
Then leaf subsides to leaf.
So Eden sank to grief,
So dawn goes down to day.
Nothing gold can stay.

-- Robert Frost

Contents

The Present

Dina suddenly appeared in the door.

"Oskar Wiznicienski is here to see you," she said. She could have used the intercom, but I encourage the human touch. I closed the folder on my desk, information about random access memory, and put it away. I want my clients to remember that they are my only concern.

"Oskar!"

"Menachem!"

"Come in, sit down. You're looking fine."

He is a wiry man about the size of a leprechaun. His complexion is pink, healthy, his eyes almost merry, and his energy quite daunting. But for a man as rich as he is--and I know to the penny how much he is worth--he dresses in surprisingly shabby clothes. Blue serge suit pants, vintage 1950s, with a shiny seat. A long-sleeved white shirt, even in summer, slightly frayed at the collar points. I've become accustomed to the eccentricities of the rich.

"Can I get you something to drink, Mr. Wiznicienski?"

"Is this on the account, Menachem?"

"No Oskar, it's free."

"Then I'll have a glass of orange juice, Dina, not cold."

"Menachem?"

"Coffee."

"So, Menachem, I hear you're going to Poland."

"Yes. Germany first."

"Germany?"

"It came as a surprise to me, too. The German embassy got in touch. The city of Freiburg invites everyone displaced by the war to return for a commemorative visit, at their expense, and to dedicate a memorial."

"I didn't know you were a Freiburger."

"That's how I got out--through the Schwarzwald into Switzerland. And now Tova and I are going back for the first time in almost fifty years."

"Wives too?"

"Everything. Air fare. Five-star hotel. Banquet with the mayor and city councilors in the Burgermeister's hall. All paid for by the German government and the city of Freiburg. A real gift. Completely unexpected."

"El Al?"

"No. Lufthansa--it's part of the deal. Zürich first and then on to Freiburg. Tova is really quite excited about Zürich. Looking forward to the duty-free shopping. Swiss chocolates, cheese. You want me to bring you presents for your grandchildren too?"

"No. I don't need you to buy anything for my grandchildren, but if you're going on to Warsaw ...."

"Yes, I am."

"... there's something you might do for me, if you have the time."

"Of course. Anything."

He laid five one-thousand dollar bills on the table.

"Give these to a man called Krysten Swoboda. If he's still alive and you can find him. He must be in his middle eighties by now."

"Who is he, a cousin? Still living there?"

"No. No relation. He took care of me during the war."

"He must have treated you like a prince. What did he do, put you up in a villa on Lake Como?"

"Ha-ha! No. I hid in the forest. But I'll tell you, Menachem, there's not much to eat in the forest for a city boy. I couldn't bring myself to eat grubs and worms. Could you? The birds were too fast and the small animals too clever. I ate nuts and roots mostly, some eggs I stole from chicken coops, fruit from orchards. But mostly I starved."

Dina came in with the orange juice and coffee.

"Thank you, Dina."

"Well, eventually they caught me not because I was a Jew but because I was a thief. Stole food from a peasant's cart. They sent me to Sachsenhausen. That's where I met Krysten Swoboda. Everyone knew who he was and he knew everyone. I arrived near the end of the war. No food. No medicine. And there was typhus in the camp. I worked. How I worked. But not even I am immune to the disease. I became ill and crawled into bed to die."

I shifted in my chair. I didn't want the coffee.

"There's something familiar and comfortable about dying," Oskar said. "Yes. You grow accustomed to the fever. The shivers make you smile. The pain in your guts is almost comfortable--I don't know, because it's not worse, maybe. That's the point. It's not unendurable. It's familiar. You lie there waiting, knowing you will either die or get better and there's not much you can do one way or the other. And it really doesn't matter."

"But you didn't die."

He smiled. "But I didn't know that then," he said, holding up a finger. "I thought I was going to die. I was waiting to die. And Krysten Swoboda came down the aisle between the bunks. I had spoken to him, maybe a day or two before. There wasn't much light and he came slowly. When he got to my bunk, he stopped for a moment to make sure no one was watching. Then he reached into his shirt and placed half a loaf of bread on my chest. Half a loaf of bread! Do you know what that meant in the camps at the end? It was a gift, you see. He gave me my life. I turned to the wall, the precious bread protected by my body beneath the blanket. I ate the bread slowly over the next few days, first the soft insides and then the crust, and I knew I was alive. A few days later we were liberated and got to eat Russian food, cabbage, potatoes."

"And now you want to pay him back."

"Now I can return the present."

"Five-thousand dollars for half a loaf of bread?"

"Well, of course, I could give more, but I have his pride to consider. Too little isn't enough and too much is an insult. Anyway, five-thousand dollars is a lot of money in Poland."

"Especially for an old man," I said.

"If he's still alive."

"I'll do it, of course," I said, smiling broadly.

"And if you see that he's impoverished and needs more, give from your own pocket. I'll pay you back when you return."

"My pleasure."

"I would do the same for you," he said.

2.

I love to fly first-class, especially when it is free. When I fly to Europe on business, the client eventually pays. But this was different. A gift. All the money was up-front, and I didn't have to wait for anything. Tickets and spending money in Deutschemarks-- not much but enough--arrived by courier from the German embassy.

And I'll tell you something else. I like to fly Lufthansa. They project the most civilized aspects of German culture. The music is Strauss and Mozart. The people are courteous. The planning is impeccable and the execution unobtrusive. The food is as good as can be expected for people confined in a small and dangerous place, surrounded by polished steel and suspended thousands of feet above the earth.

But most of all I like the cutlery. It has the elegance of German functionality and the user-friendly design of the very best German manufactures. Whenever I fly Lufthansa, I always take a knife or a spoon or a fork. They're not quite elegant or full-sized enough for everyday use, but good enough for picnics with the grandchildren. They're better than plastic, and we don't much care if a piece gets lost. They're easily replaceable. I consider it part of German reparations.

The city of Freiburg was as generous as could be expected. They met us--we were thirty-three Israelis--at the airport. They immediately separated us from the rest of the tourists, gathered us at a special collection point, waved us through customs, handled all our baggage, provided special transport direct to the hotel where, again, a special selection process eased us through registration. They had our names and country of origin on a list with room numbers already assigned. Instead of the usual hassle of hotel registration, we gave our names, and they gave us a number and a key. We were expected. All the arrangements had been made. Impeccable planning!

I remembered many of the people who came from Israel and even some of the others who came from the United States, Mexico, South America. One couple came from New Zealand. They said that was as far away as they could get and never expected to return to Freiburg.

In many ways, the best part of the trip was the banquet in the medieval Burgermeister's hall. How we ate! A feast served by waiters in medieval costume. Bright scarlet and blue silk, brass buttons, gold braid and epaulettes. Some unfortunates, of course, had food prepared especially for them by a cook flown over from a kosher hotel in Switzerland, but the rest of us ate like we've never eaten before. Such meats, such vegetables, such cakes and breads. And beer and wine and desserts like only the Germans can make.

The whole thing was impressive. The various dishes, skillfully prepared, arrived hot all at the same time. How they do that for a banquet of over one hundred people, I'll never know. A real triumph of German efficiency.

My chair was next to one of the oak pedestals on which the refectory table rested, and there, carved into the wood, was a little medieval mouse, caught forever scurrying up the table leg to get the last morsels of food before the brothers cleared it away.

3.

Then Tova returned home and I went by myself to Poland. Germany is modern; Poland is medieval. Germany is rich; Poland is impoverished. Germany is busy about the future; Poland remembers the past. It was like stepping back into the muddy Middle Ages. The markets were empty. A few shriveled carrots. Shabby cabbages. Oh yes, they have trains and heavy industry, but I always felt this was a façade imported to impress foreigners with Poland's modernity when all the time the real Poland of horse-drawn carts, sudden violence, and milking by hand was just beyond the wall. Not waiting to be discovered or changed. No. Waiting with the stolidity of the bovine to return.

After I finished my business in Warsaw, I was to return to the twentieth century by catching a LOT flight to Frankfurt and then the Lufthansa flight home. But first I went to find this Krysten Swoboda fellow for Oskar. Oh, I found him. Yes. He wasn't hard to trace. His pre-war union had merged with another and been absorbed by a third, but in all the permutations Swoboda's name remained constant. He was almost a hero, a semi-famous man. On the one hand, he was an original communist from the days before the communists came to power. Now that the communists were out, he was a fossil, an irrelevant historical anecdote. He had a government pension and had lived for many years already in a retirement home about forty miles from Warsaw.

And so on a golden day in late summer, a rented car and driver took me for a ride in the Polish country-side among wheat fields ripe for harvest so that I could deliver a gift to an old man from an old friend who remembered.

The driver knew I was a foreigner and therefore rich. He expected an enormous tip which, converted into zlotys, was worth a week's wages. He tipped his cap and opened the door obsequiously. He chattered like a child. He pointed out notable sites, former gypsy camps and Jewish villages.

"The Polish people are 97% pure now," he said proudly.

When we stopped at a traffic light, he pulled a bottle of wine from beside his seat, uncorked it with his teeth, and tipped it up. He offered me a swig, but I said "No, thanks."

The place where Swoboda had been sent to die had been the summer residence of some Polish prince, a scion of the Radziwells. It endured all the benefits of communist equality. The walls were freshly whitened with a lime-wash. The brass-and-gilt filigreed shutters were painted black. The walnut wainscoting was institutional green. Only the floor remained as it was: black and white stone squares in the foyer, old parquet in the side rooms. But the parquet was worn and varnished, not waxed, and pocked with age, neglect, indifference. Some strips had lifted off and disappeared. Each design squealed in a different voice and gave like spongy carpet as I walked across what had once been a dining-room to meet Krysten Swoboda.

I expected senility--he was near 90. I would present the money to the institution to guarantee a little better care or more food or warmer blankets for the winter and then return home in good conscience, having honored Oskar's memory of a kindness that saved his life.

But Krysten Swoboda wasn't in a wheelchair; he sat in the sun beside an open window. He stood up quite easily, I thought, and, resting on a cane, bowed slightly toward me as we were introduced. His clothes were neat though old, not shabby. What was frayed had been neatly trimmed away. The buttons were sewn with thread that looked like twine. His clothes displayed care and crispness, that same rigor of mind that must have preserved him in the war and in the camps and in the unions both before and after. I felt I was in the presence of a remarkable man--erratically wrinkled around the eyes. His brow and cheeks were smooth, pink even, like a boy's. His eyes were small and watery and blue. He wore no glasses.

"From the Holy Land?"

"Yes," I said.

"I have never been there. Nor have I ever wished to go. It was enough for me that our Lord was from that place."

"You don't mind if I ask you some questions?"

"No. I have been interviewed many times."

"I want to ask you about the war and about the time you were in Sachsenhausen."

He looked at me keenly before he said, "You Jews are only interested in the war and the camps. Yes. It was a terrible time, but no worse than any other war. The first war was worse in many ways. But you Jews only want the second war. You think it is your war."

"Many of us died, and we were civilians, not soldiers."

"Many die in all the wars and most of the dead are civilians. You must learn to forget."

"Our strength is that we remember," I said.

"A mistake. The Swedes conquered us and butchered us and now they are our friends. Then the Russians came and did the same. Then the French. Then the Germans. Each time it was terrible. But now we are all friends. The lesson of history is to forget the past. That is how we survive. Even after Pearl Harbor, the Americans are friends with the Japanese. And look at the

Germans."

"That's what I want to talk about."

"The Germans were no worse than Napoleon or the Cossacks."

"Do you remember the end of the war?"

"Yes."

"You were in Sachsenhausen."

"Yes."

"There was typhus in the camp."

"A terrible disease especially to the weak and malnourished. All were dying, prisoners and workers alike. There was no water to drink. Everything was filthy and dying. There was no food."

"And yet you gave away half a loaf of bread."

"No," he said.

The sun danced with shadow in the shredded garden. The sheer curtain stirred with the odor of wheat fields and manure.

"You didn't give a ration of bread to a sick man?"

"Never."

"Toward the end there in Sachsenhausen? Just in the last days?"

He was silent for a moment, but his clear eyes never wavered from my face.

"I know what you mean," he said at last. "I went to see Peter Kruglanski, a man from my quarter of Warsaw, who was dying of typhus. He had received his ration of bread the day before, and I wanted to see if he had eaten it. But Kruglanski was dead when I got to the workers' barracks. The loaf of bread was under his blanket, his dirty hand still stuck in it. The bread would have been found by those who came to bury him, but at the end no one worked, and the dead lay among the living until the Russians came."

"That was the bread?"

"Yes. I took it. Who else better to inherit than I, his friend from Warsaw. I put it in my shirt."

"Then why did you give it away?"

"Yes. I was hungry, you see, but not starving. Even at the end I had some privilege and was not prepared to eat rotting potato peel--like some. I was still in the workers' barracks, among the dead and the dying. The stench was awful. The lights were erratic because of the Russian advance. The electricity went on and off and on. And as I walked between the rows of corpses, I thought 'This bread is surely contaminated. If I eat it, I will die.' It was yesterday's bread, you see, in the dirty hands of a man dead from typhus in the barracks where the very air was poisonous to breathe. I took the bread out of my shirt and left it on the chest of a dead man there. I didn't give it away; I threw it away. Anyone willing to take contaminated bread off the body of a dead man could have it as far as I was concerned."

"Two days later the Russians arrived?"

"Yes. Two or three days. I don't remember. And when the Russians arrived, we ate like princes! Such feasting! Soup made from cabbage and potatoes. Tea with sugar. A little beet borscht. I have never eaten so happily or so well."

"Do you remember Oskar Wiznicienski?"

"No."

"He also survived in the workers' barracks until the Russians came."

"I don't remember everyone."

"A Jew," I said.

"Really? A Jew? Then what was he doing in the workers' barracks? It was not allowed."

"He was imprisoned as a thief, not as a Jew. He was the one you gave the bread to."

"Impossible." He sat quite still. "I put the contaminated bread on the body of a dead man." He leaned forward in his chair and looked me evenly in the eye.

"I would never have given that bread to a Jew," he said.

The Present

...t in the driveway beyond the garden, my driver was ...lishing his ancient car in erratic sunlight. He saw me watching through the window and gaily waved his snotty handkerchief.

Avshalom showere
body and, although i⸱
came out of the b⸱
bedroom, towel⸱
open second⸱
orchard o⸱
rising i⸱
lane
da⸱

day.
off wei⸱
pair. He tra⸱.
clean shorts and
hall gritty with sand
the wind blowing and
otherwise.

"Mmmm, there's a good sm⸱
for the salad.

"You smell like strawberries in suns⸱

damp from the day and the cooking.

"Well," she laughed, turning down the fire under the noisy eggs, "I'll smell better after I've finished cooking, had a shower, and put the other two to bed."

"You're not coming with me, Hami?"

"No," said Nechama, rinsing her hands, "you can relive your past by yourself. I'll be the clean-smelling girl in your bed when you return."

"I'm not reliving my past," he protested. "Stacy and I were in college together."

"There's no lover like a Harvard lover," she said, kissing him properly. "I know from my experience."

"Come on. She married Eric, after all. Not me."

"The roommate who died."

There was no response to that. Avshalom had a cold surprise when he saw Eric's name in the shiny alumni magazine which, together with elegant and articulate requests for financial contributions, the college sent with depressing regularity into this windswept collection of stony fields and ragged orchards in Israel.

He had read her the brief obituary.

Class of '88. Eric Percival Zilbersteen. November 10, in Brookline, MA, suddenly by misadventure. He was the theater and film reviewer for the Boston *Globe* and winner of the Pelham King Award for Short Fiction. Married in 1990 to the former Stacy Borsowitz (class of '89), he also leaves his parents, and a brother.

"So now her husband's dead and she's come here," Nechama continued. She took three tomatoes from the basket on the counter.

"It's one of those whirl-wind tours, Hami. Stacy didn't come to see me."

"Funny that she should come to see her husband's good old college roommate only after her husband has died," said Nechama, cutting tomatoes for the salad.

"What's funny about that? Most Diaspora Jews come sooner or later. It's a way of saying they're Jewish."

"But she wrote you that letter," said Nechama, scraping the cut tomatoes into the salad bowl.

"Yes."

"Now she just wants to see you and ask something," said Nechama, stripping an onion of its skin.

"That's what she said. Probably something about Eric. I don't know."

"And you're going to see her," said Nechama, cutting into the onion.

"It's just here in Tel Aviv. You saw her schedule. This is the only time she's free."

"Have a nice time reliving your past," Nechama said, the knife flashing the onion into tiny shards.

"Hey! Are you crying?"

"Don't be silly. It's the onion," she said brightly.

2.

They escaped from the garish lobby of the Daniel Hotel with its grotesque chandeliers and shiny surfaces into the more subdued light of the bar.

"This is more like it," Stacy Zilbersteen said as they sat on low-slung tufted love seats in a corner by the darkened window. They sat on opposite sides of a low square table. A candle burning in a faceted crystal lamp was the only light between them. He sat back and crossed one bare leg over the other in a T. His dusty sandal dangled. She sat sideways on the leading edge of her seat, her pleated skirt falling in a graceful white arc from her knees to the floor in exactly the same arc that her smooth golden hair made falling from her forehead to her shoulder.

As he looked at her over the crescent rim of his Goldstar beer,

Avshalom tried to determine what made Stacy so American, what gave her, even in the dead heat of August, that blend of New England crispness, Boston grace, and Cambridge polish. He decided it was her escape from weather. Buffered from birth against discomfort, she assumed all rooms would be centrally heated against the cold and air conditioned against the summer's heat. That American assumption gave her an air of energetic eagerness and a readiness to open new worlds with an iron wedge.

"So you're a kibbutz farmer now," she said.

He explained the difference between moshav and kibbutz and said, "but I am a farmer."

"Who ever would have thought when we left Harvard, Teddy, that you would be a farmer? You, of all people. It seems so ... the antithesis of your spiritual potential. You were so socially committed. I remember when you taught English to Mexican migrant workers one summer and then worked as a guard in an integrated inner-city school in the Back Bay. Whatever became of your commitment to the impoverished and the dispossessed?"

"Now I teach English to impoverished avocados," Avshalom laughed, "and guard the dispossessed eggplant. With about the same rate of success, I might add."

She laughed too, but she also persisted. "And you wrote so beautifully."

He demurred with a smile.

"I was so proud," she went on, "when the American Repertory Theater put on 'When Soft Was the Sun,' a play by Ted Danziger at The Loeb. And Robert Brustein wanted to take it to New York. Even the *Crimson* loved it," she said, as though that were the ultimate accolade.

"Well, they had to, didn't they?" Avshalom laughed. "Eric wrote the review. He knew if he didn't praise the play, I would short-sheet his bed and put frogs in it."

Stacy laughed too in that echoing musical way she had.

So they talked about Eric and his pointless death--a city death by kids wilding at Revere Beach. Instead of giving up his wallet, he tried to talk to them about improving their lives. Avshalom recognized Eric's disengaged, intellectual, liberal Jewish reaction that typically led him to sympathize with the migrants, the impoverished, the damaged, the homeless, and the Palestinians. So as he was talking, they knocked him down and stomped him.

"You never had any children?" Avshalom asked.

"No. You remember how he was. Managing Eric's life was a full-time job. I had no time for children." Then she turned her golden smile upon him. "But you're married too, I hear."

"Yes."

"Do you have any children?" she asked.

"Two of each."

"And your wife?"

"She has two of each, too," he laughed.

"No, I meant ...."

"Her name is Nechama. Hami."

"What sort of name is that?" Stacy wanted to know.

"A standard sort of Israeli name. It means Consolation. I have an Israeli name, too," he said.

"What's Israeli about Theodore Danziger?"

"Well, my name's Avshalom Golani now."

"What? Avshalom Go-what?" She was upset. "Why do you have a new name?"

"You took a new name when you got married," he said. "You abandoned the Son of Bors to become the Silver Stone."

She was incredulous.

"Why ever would you want a new name?"

"It's part of the prehistoric ritual for entering a new life." He went on, amused at her disbelief. "New name. New clothes. New life. It's official. Passport and everything."

"Well, let me tell you, it hasn't been very funny for me to enter into my new life," she said. "I'm a widow now. My life is lonely--and I don't like to be alone."

She paused, remembering.

"Oh, sure, after Eric died our friends would come over to extend their condolences. The couples were an affront to me, as if Eric's death were something that I had done wrong which they were trying to convince me to correct. The women invariably talked while the husbands invariably lingered. And then one husband or the other would stop by on his way home from work to fix a leaking this or broken that and would offer to service me as if being a widow were somehow a return to an undesirable virginity."

He raised his glass to signal the waitress for another beer.

"But that's not what being a widow really is," Stacy said. "Being a widow is like being born again."

Avshalom raised his eyebrows and looked at her.

"I was suddenly free," she went on. "I could do whatever I wanted, go anywhere, see anyone I pleased, without having to answer to any other person in the whole world. I was overwhelmed by the opening up of my life. It was--it is--exhilarating. Free. Absolutely and completely free. You have no idea what that is."

Avshalom absolutely looked at her being completely free.

"And I was free to do things a second time. Bobby Frost was wrong. I can choose both ways and be one person. I can live my whole life over again if I want."

So here it comes, he thought.

"And you've decided to start here in Israel," he said.

"Yes," she said. "I thought I would start with you."

"Something you wanted to ask me."

"Yes. I want you to come back with me. I know you have talent. I'm convinced you have genius. I want you to know that it's not too late."

"To do what?" he asked.

"To start again. With me. The way it was always supposed to

be. You owe it to yourself to achieve the fame you were born to achieve."

"Soooo," he said evenly--and then added with seeming inappropriateness, "Is this your first trip to Israel?"

Stacy considered quickly before she admitted, "I was here for about fourteen hours in 1990."

"Fourteen hours? With Eric?"

"No, before I married. I landed at Lod and took a cab to Sasa, the driver didn't know where it was, and then once I got there--it took about five hours--no one knew where you had gone."

Avshalom looked at her for a moment before he continued as though he were asking about her tour.

"What have you seen in Israel this time?"

"Oh, everything," she said, dismissing the irrelevant.

"Yes," he smiled ironically. "It's one of the advantages of a small country. You can see everything in a short time."

"Well, I have seen everything," she insisted. And then she paused. "I'll never understand how you could have left what you had in the states to come here, to bury your talent in the desert. And change your way of life. Even change your name."

Stacy looked at him keenly, trying to pierce his rumpled shirt, his dusty, scruffy sandals, to get to the skin she once had memorized. They were sitting in the subdued light of a bar that could have been overlooking the sea in Swampscott or Marblehead. They were surrounded by people wearing American clothes, drinking American drinks.

"The Ted Danziger I remember," she continued, "loved music and books. He wrote dialogue like an angel. He had the chance to open a play on Broadway when he was twenty-one. And instead, you disappeared. You left all this," she spread her arms, "for ... for a frightful desert filled with soldiers with guns and Arabs who want to kill you. It's dangerous and terrifying, the opposite end of the world from Boston. How could you have?"

Since it was a question that required no answer, he sipped his beer.

"Don't you remember who you were?"

"I know who I am," he said.

"I know who you used to be," she insisted. "But I don't know who you are anymore. You're not the man I thought you were."

"I never was the man you thought I was."

"I thought you loved me once," she said.

"I did."

"So what happened?"

"I fell in love with ...."

"Nechama?"

"Well, yes, but I was going to say that I fell in love with this country first."

Again, she looked at him with incredulity.

"You fell in love with a country?" she said. "With this country? This dirt-poor, rocky, hot, unbearable, wounded country where nothing grows but stones? You're joking."

He looked at his watch. Not far from where he was joking, the sprinklers among the fig trees would be shutting down. Water was collecting at the end of the glistening leaves, gathering in the lobes, and dropping silently into the night. And the ground lines among the red and green bell peppers would engorge with water now and drip into the wounded fields.

"And its history. And its people. And its calendar," Avshalom continued.

"We have history, people, and a calendar in the United States, too," she said.

"What do I care," he said in return, "about the Battle of Cowpens or the Viet Nam war? The Tingaling Indians or Halloween?"

"You have family in the states."

He paused before he said, "It's only biological."

She was not to be convinced.

"How can you possibly love a country more than a person?"

"Ahhh," he said.

"What do you mean, 'ahhh'?"

"Here we see," he said, uncrossing the T he had made with his legs, "the fundamental Romanticism of our education. We learned to privilege the sanctity of the individual above everything else."

"I don't understand," she said.

Avshalom sat forward on the well-worn love seat. "Remember that ethical nugget we used to delight in when we were children in college? How did it go? 'If ever I am presented with the choice of betraying my country or my friend, I hope to God I have the courage to betray my country.'"

"So?" she responded. "I still believe in the sanctity of the individual. I only have one life to live and it's going to be the best I can possibly make it for me. And you have only one life to live too, Ted, and you're throwing it away in the desert."

"But I no longer think friendship more important than patriotism," he said. "Here I could never betray my country."

"You already betrayed your country by coming here."

"But this is my country," he said.

She could only say, "I'll never understand how you could possibly choose this country over your genius--over me and everything I have to share with you. Money. Security. Boston--and the life we could live there. And the chance to achieve the fame you were born to achieve."

"I know," he said.

She looked at him perplexed. "What do you know?" she asked.

"You'll never understand."

3.

He turned off the road to Tulkarm, away from the sparkling

hillside before him, and on to the black secondary road until he came to the crushed stone road that led toward the moshav. The headlights of the car drowned out the starlight and made the night seem black. The gate was still open, but Avram had just come up and was standing by to close and lock it behind him. Avshalom stopped the car beside his father-in-law.

"A good evening, Avshi," said Avram, smiling at the strange American his daughter had chosen to marry. "Everything okay?"

"Hey, grandfather," Avshalom said in greeting. "Do you want Tzvi and Daphna to help with the flowers tomorrow?"

"I need everyone I can get. Send Dror and Noa, too."

"Six and four?" Avshalom laughed. "But they can never be too young to help with the harvest, can they?"

"Igal's home," Avram said.

The two men smiled at each other. They knew what it was to be home from Lebanon.

"Every day a miracle," Avram said.

"See you tomorrow," said Avshalom as Avram stood back from the car and waved him into the safety of the community.

He drove carefully. Though the road within the moshav was paved, it fell off sharply into drainage ditches on both sides. There were no streetlights, but yellow lamplight or the blue light from television sets marked where the houses were.

He pulled into the drive and turned off the engine. Only then was he aware of the noise it had made. He stood a moment beside the creaking car as it settled down for the night. He waited for his eyes to become accustomed to darkness and his ear attuned to the night--the racket of crickets, the belching of frogs, the buzz of insects, and the swing of the wing of owl and bat busy about the night's slaughter. Behind the house, a domestic cat crept stealthily along the line between the trim grass and the field, paused, and carefully entered the taller grass beyond.

As usual, the back door was open and a small light glowed

above the stove. He scrunched up the stairs and looked in on the sleeping children before making his way to the bedroom.

"Hi," said Nechama in a low night voice.

"Hi," he whispered as he sat on her side of the bed.

"How was it?"

"Okay."

"What did she want?"

"Stacy? She reminded me of something I have to do."

"What?"

"Nothing important. I'll tell you about it in the morning."

"Mmmmnh."

"Night."

"Night," she said.

"You smell good," he said.

She reached a warm arm out from under the sheet, hooked his neck, and drew him to her. He kissed her gently.

As he came out through the back of the house, he took a mattock from the tumble of tools leaning against the toolshed in the garden. The crumbling cardboard box he wanted was in the lower left-hand drawer of the worktable in the shed where he repaired small motors and faulty tools.

He swung down the lane away from the house, past the avocado orchard and the mango trees. His feet were cool in the black air of the lane wet with dew as the earth absorbed the cold starry sky. The potato or the onion fields would not do because of the way they were harvested, but somewhere among the tangle of melons he stopped and dug a hole. The mattock blade flashed in the moonlight as it plunged again and again into the loamy earth. He put the decaying box into the hole and covered it over with dirt.

Before the field was harrowed, the worms would find it out. By the end of the year, with the first rains, it would begin to molder and rot. It would soak in the heavier winter rains that fell between Hanukkah and Purim. Before Pesach and the spring flowers, all the decrepit words he had written would dissolve and run together. By Remembrance Day and Independence Day, they would melt into the stony soil.

As he stood from his labor, he looked out toward the small dark stand of trees, close to him now, at the end of the lane where the moonlight was shining on the sillion the tractor raised. In the starry light, he could just make out the jagged outline beneath the trees.

White stones set perpendicular to the earth.

The year each stone was planted had been carefully marked.

And each stone had a name.

One stone bore the name of Nechama's husband who did not return from Lebanon.

Mothers

For Helena Rapp, 1977--25 May, 1992. And for all the others.

I'm done with crying now. It's over. No more to cry for. Soon they will come for me.

We heard them coming. My mother held me trembling against her trembling breast because she could do no more than hold me there in the cold Dutch morning. Her fingers clenched at my back, snagged in my braids. The smell of her (is that what it was?--the stench of her?--or was it the horses?) *and the trickle of fear that stained the front of her blouse.*

They dragged us from the cupboard abandoned in the barn behind the house, boys little older than I was then, old men much older than I ever hoped to be. Their guns kept falling over. Sliding down their arms on the straps.

"Out," they said. "Jews out." But their hearts weren't in it. They were doing it for their country.

My heart isn't in ...

My heart isn't ...

"Stand there," they said.

I couldn't stand. My legs were cramped with the cupboard and the cold. Mother held me. She held me.

I can't stand now. Shira's lying somewhere, too. Where is she? Why can't I ... hold ... her?

They should have shot us. It was the law. It would have been better.

They told us to stand, wait against the barn, but the truck didn't come for us.

It will not come here. The truck. The truck will not come here. No. They don't let the truck come here.

We stood against the wooden wall under a gray sky, cold for May in Holland and the wind coming. All morning we stood and the rain came. But the truck didn't come. They sheltered against the rain in the woodshed and the dovecote. We stood under the eaves of the barn with the wind blowing the cold rain about us, the wet hem of my dress cold against my leg.

Not here in the heat.

Not here in the sun.

Not this May.

Not now.

No.

The truck didn't come. It was getting dark, with the rain from the gray skies, and the truck didn't come. So they left. Slowly. In groups. With their rifles slung over their drooping shoulders. They were going home, the old men and the boys. Because the truck didn't come for the Jews. They left us.

We ran.

To another country.

Where it never rains. Where the white sun warms the white stone that covers my mother ...

There's no one left.

Shira was the last.

Soon they will come for me.

I must ...

I must get up now.

Wash my face.

Change my dress.

Not in the bathroom.

No.

It's against the law, and I can't.

I ... can't.

Slowly.

So as not to wake ...

As if there were anyone to ...

Yes, I can wash my ...

In the kitchen.

The water was always cold in Holland when I was her age. To drink. To bathe. It smelled of iron. My mother washed me in water that smelled of iron. I washed Shira in water that tasted of heat.

The smell of iron? Here?

On the knife blade.

They should have shot us. The trucks should have come.

The buses came. The children piled in. One of the buses wouldn't start. And those children had to ride with the others, crowding three and four to a pair of seats while some sat on their backpacks in the aisle. Such laughing. Such singing. My ears hurt. Class *bar mitzvah* on Masada. All the sixth-grade classes.

We slept in Arad, and she climbed the ramp first in the morning. Shira was first of all the girls when she climbed the ramp. She was there with the girls waving and singing when the boys came singing with the Torah up the ramp to Masada.

In the morning.

Two years ago?

And the hot wind ringing and the hot dust blowing through the windy stony remnant of a synagogue.

There too. Yes. It was there, too. Once.

And with knives.

Almost two o'clock.

Turn on the ...

She's there.

I know she'll be there.

"*Kol Yisrael M'Yerushalaim. Shalom Rav*--This is the Voice of Israel, speaking from Jerusalem. Good afternoon. It is now two o'clock. Here is the news, read by Adi Tadmore. The funeral of fifteen-year-old Shira Sadka--*zichrona l'vracha*--stabbed to death on her way to school this morning will be held at the cemetery in Bat Yam at 2:30. The terrorist from Gaza, apprehended at the scene, is in stable condition at Ichilov Hospital."

Yes.

They're coming for me now.

It's time to go.

Roots

The food was not quite right. Jason wasn't accustomed to breakfast of sliced silver herring over poached egg on toast and a cream-filled brioche topped with hot chocolate sauce sprinkled with chopped walnuts. So he traded with Karen: she took the herring--the Danes were hardy, sea-faring stock and accustomed to impossible breakfasts--and, though he was not quite happy about the cholesterol, he took the eggs. Both gave their cream brioches to Colin, the twin who was at the age when he would eat anything. Felicity, the twin at the age when she would eat nothing, drank coffee and picked at a corner of toast.

The El Al flight from LA to Frankfurt was okay though Jason was disappointed not to find the kind of Jewish food he was accustomed to have on Sunday mornings at Canter's. The food on the LOT flight to Warsaw was more Solidarity than tasty. And no food at all was served on Aeroflot to Riga. It seemed to reflect the breakup of the former Soviet Union.

Only now as the train rumbled (it really rumbled) up the Gulf of Riga toward Tallinn did he feel that the food was actually prepared for him personally rather than packaged anonymously in some food factory to be microwaved at thirty-six thousand feet. But the food, when it arrived, was disappointing. The colors were wrong. The bacon was thick, white, translucent; the eggs were orange; the cream yellow. Though it tasted better than it looked, it was not quite what he thought he ordered and not quite what he expected.

But then the whole trip was not quite right. Before the twins went off to junior college in the fall, he wanted to give them some sense of where the Motlis family came from and who they were. This might be their last summer together. Already the family was starting to pull apart, Colin to Mendocino and Felicity to Fullerton. Jason wanted Felicity to go farther from home where she might learn to be independent and get away from Mark, but Karen led him to see that the choice wasn't his. Nonetheless, he impressed upon Felicity that we all have to live with the choices we make.

Colin was easier, still malleable. But his mind was more on the week of JV practice he would miss in mid-summer than on the limpid gulf opening to their left under a lowering sky the color of water and, to their right, the ripening green fields rolling toward the silver morning and opening eastward upon all the golden Russias.

"What are you thinking about, Jason?"

He smiled at his wife. The morning light behind her made a nimbus of her golden hair.

"Whenever you get that look in your eyes," continued Karen, "I know you're up to something. "

"Oh, the towns we passed. The romance of names. Saulkrasti, Salacgriva, Ainazi, Kilingi-Nomme .... "

"How much farther do we have to go, dad? "

"We get off at Pärnu. Next stop, I think. And from there we'll take a bus or a taxi to Sindi. Grandpa Alex used to say it was twelve kilometers and a good morning's walk."

"What's that in, like, real distance?"

"About eight miles, Colin."

"Grandpa walked it every day?"

"No, once a week. He and his mother would come with a wagonload of whatever was ripe on the farm and sell it in the market at Pärnu. It was the nearest big town."

"Define 'big.'"

"Oh, I don't know, Felicity, maybe ten thousand in the nineteen thirties."

"Wow! Ten thousand people! Almost enough to fill a whole basketball stadium."

Colin snickered.

"Don't get smart, young lady."

"What's been your favorite part of the vacation so far, Felissie?" Karen asked.

"I liked Germany. Germany's great. All those castles on the Rhine are so beautiful. I mean, you can just imagine being a princess there. Looking out. Being serenaded by knights in shining armor."

"One of them named Mark D'Amato," Colin sneered.

"Mother!"

"What did you like best, Colin?"

"So far?--the '62 Citroën DS that picked us up at the hotel in wherever. Talk about a Princess, man, that was a real classy car. Hydraulic self-leveling. Button for a brake. Beats the ID model, hands down."

"Grandpa Alex didn't have a car," Jason interposed before Colin became enthusiastic. "When he got to Philadelphia, he bought a horse and wagon so he could go into the only business he knew."

"Why didn't he buy a car?"

"People didn't have cars in those days, Colin. And he was poor. Remember, he didn't have all the advantages you've had."

"He could have bought a *used* car."

"Grandpa Alex had a horse in the back yard and fed it hay and cleaned out the stable every day."

"Did you ride the horse, dad?"

"No, Felicity. That was before I was born."

Felicity turned and spoke softly, as if to her reflection in the window.

"Why am I being told all this?"

Karen answered: "So that you'll know something about your roots."

"About my Jewish roots," said Felicity. "What about my Danish roots? How come you never tell us stories about growing up in Skibby? At least you were there."

2.

The Hotel Polonia in Pärnu showed traces of old-world class not yet resurrected from the depredations of Soviet egalitarianism. The marble staircase curved gracefully up from the empty lobby, but the iron pins used to repair it had stained the marble with rust. The rooms were large and airy with both newly silvered steam-heat radiators and a wood-burning fireplace set in ceramic tile. French windows opened on to a tiny useless balcony with wrought-iron balustrade overlooking the bay. No comparison to the Ramada Renaissance in Frankfurt.

The concierge engaged a car for them to make the trip to Sindi and a driver reputed to understand English. After an extravagant buffet of hot, peculiar food, without cereal or low-fat yogurt, they were led out of the hotel dining room and introduced to an enormously tall man who had thick whorls of unkempt hair under his cap and large clumps of successful secondary growth luxuriating in ears and nostrils. They couldn't keep their eyes off his nose until he smiled and revealed a shocking absence of teeth. He looked like a nine-foot three-year old. They referred to him in whispers as the Handsomest Driver in Pärnu.

His car, a late model Skoda, held five uncomfortably, and the ride to Sindi, at first through industrial Pärnu, was ugly.

"Great scenery, dad."

Soon the road opened on to fields of alfalfa and ryegrass

waving under low gray skies with clumps of dark forest scattered over the countryside.

Sindi itself was not quite satisfactory. Jason thought the Lutheran church on the town square was much plainer than an Estonian cathedral ought to have been. The City Hall was an early twentieth-century brick edifice that lacked medieval charm. The cobblestone streets were paved with asphalt.

"What are we going to do here, dad?"

"Let's walk around for a bit, Colin. Check it out."

Felicity looked about.

"I've seen it," she said.

"Your grandfather was born here in this town."

"Yeah? Well, I know why he left."

"Why?"

"No grass."

"Nothing for the horse to eat," added Colin.

It was true. As they walked through the town, all the houses seemed to start at the sidewalk, when there was a sidewalk, or at the curb. If shutters were open, curtains were drawn against peering eyes. Heavy doors of fitted oak hung upon jambs and swung upon strap-hinges of medieval iron dressed with rivets.

"Isn't that Hebrew?" Karen asked. She pointed at the weathered letters carved into the wooden architrave framing the doorway.

"Yes," said Jason. "Well, now," he said brightly to the others, "you see, this was a Jewish house. Jews lived here in ancient times."

"Can you read it, dad?"

Jason stepped on to the doorsill and looked at the inscription arching above him.

"No. Can't make out the letters. It's a blessing of some sort. Jews always bless their visitors."

"Maybe grandpa Alex lived here as a boy."

"No," said Jason, "Grandpa Alex always talked about the house by the mill. Let's see if we can find that."

They wandered inconsequentially around the small town until, with the help of their driver, they found the mill house. Set in a hollow by a river rushing toward the Gulf of Riga, it was a beautiful grange of elegant proportions, made of red and black brick. Beneath the lintel, with cornice over, hung a wavy window of delicately leaded tracery. Many chimneys, no two the same, rose in twisting columns of brick from ten or twelve places among the gables.

"Now this is more like it."

"Hey-hey!"

"Look at this," said Felicity. She pointed to pink marble set in the red brick gatepost and incised with the single word, "Motlis."

"Hey, it's like our name."

"Can we go in, dad?"

"I don't see why not. We're tourists."

"Maybe we own it. What do you think, dad?"

"It's probably the name of the house rather than the people who live here now."

The Handsomest Driver in Pärnu held the gate for them. As they stood before the lovely earthenware house, Jason noticed the gravel path that led through the vegetable garden to the fish ponds on the right of the house. Since that direction offered a better prospect of the whole house and the colorfully decorated outbuildings behind, they followed it and came upon the old woman who might be his relative.

She was sitting on a raked gravel path in a wheeled chair facing the afternoon sun. Her hair was tucked into a broad-brimmed straw hat. The shawl and the afghan across her knees were knitted by hand.

"Explain to her," said Jason to the driver, "that we're the Motlis family from Los Angeles and that we've come to visit the place where my father, Alex Motlis, was born. And ask her would she mind if we sort of looked around?"

The driver approached her, holding his cap in his hands, and, as if to speak to her more nearly on her level, dropped to his knees beside her chair. He spoke earnestly, one hand holding his cap upon his heart, the other turned towards them in offering. Only when he had finished speaking and stood up, backing away with drooping shoulders and a slight nod to his head, did she raise her eyes and her stark white face to look at them.

Jason approached her with his most ingratiating smile, designed to win the hearts and melt the minds of the most resistant buyers. But she wasn't looking at him.

"Alexei!" she barked in a surprisingly loud voice. *"Chodz tu!"*

Her bony finger pointed to the spot where the driver had kneeled. Her brows were knotted, the muscles of her face rigid.

Jason turned to the driver in confusion.

"Your son Alexei?"

"Colin," said Jason.

"She will speak your son," he said.

"Alexei! Gdzie jest zlota solniczka ktora dal Ksiaze Vladislav memu ojcu?"

"She want salt," said the driver.

"So somebody give her salt. What's this got to do with ...?"

"She want salt-cup prince Vladislav gave her father. Golden salt-cup."

"Alexei!" she cried and reached toward Colin.

Karen stepped between her son and the skeletal claw.

"I think we'd better go now, Jason."

"Yes. Thank her for us, please," he said to the driver, shepherding his family, backing away from the ferocious impotence of the old woman. As Karen and the children walked briskly up the path through the garden, Jason paused to turn and gaze again, longingly, possessively, upon the house where his father was born.

3.

Now that was disappointing. What a shame to be thwarted by a senile old woman from getting inside the house itself. They looked for a place to have a snack, finally pausing for tea (there was no Diet Coke) at a small bakery which set tiny round tables on the sidewalk in front of the shop.

Jason kept looking over his shoulder toward the mill house. Then Karen crooked an arm around his neck and, with a kiss to his cheek, took the children into the Lutheran church while he sat beside his second cup of tea. When they came out of the church, they turned away from where he sat and went toward the public fountain, a multi-purpose combination of horse-trough, public water distribution center, and war memorial. The children predictably splashed each other.

That's when he decided to take them to Auschwitz.

"What's Auschwitz, dad?"

"It's in Poland, Colin, near Cracow."

"I've heard that name before. Isn't it one of those places?"

"Yes, Felicity."

"Ugh. I don't think I want to go there."

"One of what places?" Colin asked.

"A graveyard or something," said Felicity. "A place where all the Jews were buried a hundred years ago."

"Not exactly. It's where the Jews were killed in the second world war. But more important, it's where all my aunts and uncles died."

"I didn't know you had aunts and uncles, daddy. Who were they? What were their names?"

"Well, I don't know, Felicity. They all died in Auschwitz. And all the cousins I never had, too. And their children."

"What are we going to do in a graveyard?" Colin wanted to know.

"Find out about it," said Jason. "I think it's more like a walk-through museum now."

"I don't see why we have to go to a place where there's a lot of dead people we don't even know," said Felicity.

"We're going to pay our respects," said Jason.

"But if you don't know their names," Felicity insisted, "I mean, what's the point?"

"It's important to remember that people killed Jews here and that some of them were your relatives."

"But if I never knew them, who cares?"

"A graveyard," said Colin. "Cool."

"Why are you telling me all this?"

"Because it's important, Felicity. Because I feel as though I'm losing my past and I want you, at least, to know your roots."

"That's your trip, dad, not mine. You're the one with the roots. I'm American."

"Well, I hope you get a different idea when we go to Auschwitz, Felicity. You'll see what grandpa Alex was escaping from just so that you could be born. I'm sure it will be interesting. You'll like it."

"I'll love it," said Colin, "if we get to ride in the Citroën again."

4.

The car that took them from the Hotel Russe in Cracow to Auschwitz was an Italian Fiat, quite ordinary and not at all air-conditioned. And to make matters delicate, Karen had thrown up her breakfast and Felicity was in the bad days of her period. The only thing good to be said for the day was that the sun was shining in a brisk wind when they pulled into the parking lot at

Auschwitz.

"Oh, good," said Colin as they approached the large administration building, "a restaurant."

"Not for me, please," said Karen.

"We'll stop there later, Colin. You just had breakfast."

They by-passed the restaurant and book shop and came out into an avenue of many graveled paths. They didn't know where to go at first and wandered along the stony paths among the red-brick buildings. Each building had a number.

"There are so many paths," said Karen.

"You can't get lost in Auschwitz," said Jason. "Look, let's meet over there by the bookstore in an hour."

"Dad?"

"Yes, Felissie?"

"What's a birkenau?"

"A what?" asked Colin.

"The arrow over there points to the birkenau. I just wondered what it was."

"I think it's a suburb," said Jason. "Look, kids, just stick around here in Auschwitz. Don't wander beyond the fence. We'll meet in an hour and buy some souvenirs. And get a snack," he added for Colin.

They saw the inside of the pretty, red-brick barracks.

They saw the photographs of life
in the camp.

They saw the mock-up
of the crematorium.

They saw the collection of suitcases
and shoes
and glasses.

They saw the doctor's office
and the examination rooms.

They saw the window-boxes of cheerful geraniums

on the modern, gray-stucco guesthouse.

In the middle of the morning, Colin met Felicity sitting on a bench. He sat beside her.

"So this is the place where they killed the Jews," he said.

She didn't answer.

"Why did they do it?"

"What am I, your teacher?" she said. "*Ask him.*"

"I'll tell you one thing," he said, "I'm glad I'm only half-Jewish."

"Why?"

"I'm half-dead."

She smiled at that.

"This isn't a vacation," said Felicity, "it's a history lesson."

They sat together in the comfortable silence that the twins sometimes shared.

"I'll be glad to get back," she said at last.

"You can say that again."

"I miss Mark."

"I'm missing football practice."

"Mark's better than football practice," she smiled.

"Well," Colin said, standing up. "Better get back to it."

"Yeah," she said, not moving. "I think he's going to give us a quiz at the end."

"Have you been in number eleven?" Colin asked cheerfully.

"No," she said.

"It's a really neat torture chamber," he said.

When Jason and Karen came to the bookstore, Felicity and Colin were already sitting on the bench outside.

"Have you been inside yet? Come on, lazy bones."

"I'll pass on this one, dad," she said.

"What's the matter with you? Don't you want to know your roots and what happened to your family?"

"This is boring, daddy."

"Don't you want to discover where you come from?"

"I come from Yorba Linda, daddy. I was born there."

"Me too," said Colin.

Karen touched her husband's shoulder and said, "She's not feeling well today, Jason."

"Oh," he said.

Karen and Jason did the bookstore together.

When they came out, holding hands, Colin and Felicity were playing frisbee on the grass.

They shared a bench in the sun with a sour old man, hands mounded on the knob of his cane, and watched the children play. Jason's arm lay on the back of the bench. Suddenly, he gave her a gentle hug. Karen smiled and responded by laying her head, briefly, on his shoulder. The breeze blew a strand of her fine yellow hair across his eyes.

"Colin's good," he said. "A natural athlete."

"Such a beautiful day," she enthused. "Almost California. And look. The grass is so green and well-tended here; the flower beds are so pretty. Such pretty pansies and violets, so nicely arranged."

The old man got up.

"If the grass had been here fifty years ago," he said, "I would have eaten it."

Well, what a foolish old man, they said. Imagine! Eating grass!

They called Colin and Felicity and walked down the path toward the gate to the parking lot. A group of school children about the age of the twins approached them, weeping. They wore tee-shirts that said in Hebrew and English "Walk for Life," "March of the Living," "Always Remember," and "Never Again." They carried blue and white flags of various sizes. Some of the boys were plunging the sticks that held the little Israeli flags into the grass or wedging them into the bars of the benches.

"There's a law against that in America," Colin said softly.

"There ought to be one here, too," Felicity added.

Jason and his family stood politely aside on the path to let the larger group pass. A girl with shining face, blind from weeping, turned her streaming eyes to the sky and fell to the ground. Her friends lifted her, comforted her, and without even brushing the dust from her jeans, carried her forward into the camp.

"God! How embarrassing," said Felicity, turning away.

As they continued down the path toward the restaurant, they passed a low stone monument in front of barracks 27. Jason saw words in English and went over to read them.

"What does it say?" Karen wanted to know.

"It says 'My sorrow is continually before me,'" said Jason.

Behind the monument of golden Jerusalem stone, three Israeli flags stood out at attention, snapped taut in the fresh breeze that blew over from the direction of Birkenau.

The Orange

"I'm going for my walk, honey. Want to come?"

She looked up from her book. Standing in the middle of the living room in cut-off jeans and a stained tee-shirt, her husband looked more like a kid or a refugee than the forty-four-year-old president of an electronics company recently sold for ten million in cash plus fifteen million in stock, a willing victim in the battle of mini-conglomerates. Early in life he had won at the game of making money, and now he didn't have to play anymore. He was through with the boardroom and the factory. He had left the battlefield in Chicago and come to live in this quiet, northern suburb of Tel Aviv. And since he had all the money he needed to do whatever he wanted, he could afford to dress in rags.

"I'm not sure I want to be seen in public with you in that outfit."

"What are you talking about? These are my most disreputable clothes."

He raised his arms as if in surrender and turned slowly so she could see how faded and threadbare his clothes were. Since coming to Israel and earnestly committing himself to walking, he had lost about eighteen pounds.

"Oh, really beautiful," she said.

"Thank you, Madame. But enough admiration--are you coming or not?"

"Is this a business trip?"

"What?"

"Are you walking for exercise or pleasure?"

"My exercise is my pleasure."

"Ah-ha!" she said. "There you go again. Reconciling opposites. It may have worked for labor and management, but when you walk for exercise, I need the car to keep up with you."

"And if I walk for your pleasure, I stop in front of every shop window in town."

"And never raise a sweat."

"How can I raise a sweat if I'm standing in front of a shop window?"

"I'll tell you what, my dear. You go out and sweat as much as you like, and I'll sit here with my book, and when you come back and take a shower and put on some nice clothes and your Guccis, we can go out to dinner. We're invited to the Wellmans' at 7:30. Go out and play in the traffic now, and don't bother me anymore. And don't get killed."

With an impish salute, he turned smartly on his heels, but just as he reached the door, the buzzer sounded.

He opened the door with a smile and looked into the empty hall.

"It's the intercom," she said.

"Hello," he said brightly into the phone that connected his apartment with the front security door. "Hello?"

No one answered.

"Children playing with the intercom," she said.

"Bye, dear."

"Bye."

Gilbert Martin stepped briskly out of the cool darkness beneath his building into the blinding afternoon. The westering sun was past its great heat. The air was still and solemn with the clarity of thick crystal, presupposing languor and siesta. No dogs barked. No cars moved. Even the children had not yet come out from the shaded parking areas under the buildings to play in the afternoon sun and among the lengthening shadows.

He turned away from the little town toward the orange groves at the far end of his street. The road he wanted to walk skirted the orchards, turned sandy and climbed the hill near the cemetery, became asphalt again and ran west toward the sea. To the right lay the villas and apartment houses of the town, uniformly white in the dust. To the left, beyond an ancient house or two, lay the green fields and orchards of a pretty moshav that would eventually be swallowed as the town expanded.

The trees were already beginning to take on their coats of summer dust, and the raw new buildings of the town, softening with young wisteria and ivy, had begun to sprout window-boxes of pink geraniums and lush succulents.

When he came to the orange grove, he walked quickly on the sunny side of the road, away from the trees. He peered down the long ranks and into the shadows beneath the trees, but found no terrorists lurking there. He didn't really expect to--he lived too far from the interface with violence--but he had read enough stories to know where the terrorists like to lurk. He did, however, start a hare with immense ears who must have thought he was a predator and darted away among the orderly rows of trees.

He maintained the same brisk pace as he walked up the hill to the cemetery. He started to sweat. Coming down the other side along the fringes of the town, he saw a skinny kid wobbling on a bike too big for him. His sister ran beside him and tried to help him balance by holding the handlebars, but her position was awkward; she turned the wheel and he tumbled into the dust beside the road. He skipped away without a bruise, but he took a fistful of roadside sand and stone and hurled it in a white cloud at his fleeing sister.

High above a bell-pepper field a hawk hung motionless against the light. It seemed painted there, permanent. And then, without a wrinkle, it slipped down the sky in a gentle arc and hung again farther off.

As Gilbert came to the end of the street that marked the margin between the town and the fields, he turned down a narrow road that led back through an area of large private houses toward the center of town. Two puppies, still in their first fur, their coats seemingly too large for them, tumbled in the dust, playing with their teeth at each other's throats. A man with sharp shears looked up from pruning shrubs to watch him pass.

He swung down the narrow road, happy in the day, happy to be idle and active. He looked at all the expensive villas with their grass and gardens, secretly pleased not to be concerned with such things. His penthouse roof-garden was just enough to be amusing without being work. What a lovely day!

A white Volkswagen turned from the town onto the road ahead of him. It was coming fast. He stepped off the road onto the sandy margin and looked up in time to see the most amazing sight. An orange was miraculously, wonderfully, suspended between him and the oncoming car. It hung in the air by magic. It was beautiful, improbable, the only surprising dash of color on the white road, superimposed upon the white car between the white houses. He watched with amazement and delight.

The car screamed past with a rush of mechanical noise. The orange smacked the center of his chest with a shocking thud and, breathless, dazed, he dropped to his knees in the sand, bewildered. Stone cut into his flesh as he sat over on one leg, half-on, half-off the road. The orange lay motionless beside him. It was gashed open, bleeding.

"Damn it!" he said, as he stood up suddenly, scattering stone and sand in a cloud of white dust. He peered down the road, but the car was gone. He strode off purposefully in the direction he had come, looking for the white Volkswagen. He was going to kill the people inside.

At the end of the street where the puppies were still tumbling over each other, he saw several cars parked in front of a high house. One was a white Volkswagen, facing in the wrong direction. He put his hand on the rear bonnet to see if he could feel the heat of the engine. The bonnet was warm, but the late afternoon sun was full upon it. The other cars were equally warm, or almost so. He went up to the man with the shears who was still worrying over his shrubs.

"Excuse me," said Gilbert in Hebrew.

"Speak also English," said the man, trying to be helpful.

"Well, then," said Gilbert, relieved, "you may remember that I just walked down this road here, maybe five minutes ago."

The man nodded.

"Between then and now, did this Volkswagen come up this road?"

The man continued to nod.

"Then why is it facing the opposite direction? Ah! I get it. The car came up this way and turned around so to be facing the way it had come. Very clever. Do you have a telephone?"

"Telephone? Yes." He led the way into his house.

"I want to call the police," said Gilbert.

"The police?" The man suddenly looked sober. He put down his pruning shears.

"You didn't happen to see who got out of the car, did you?"

"What?"

"Who was driving?"

"No. None."

Gilbert spoke to the police, turning once to ask the man, "what's the address here?"

"Sixty-four Yehuda HaNassi," said the thoughtful man.

"Sixty-four Yehuda HaNazzi. That's right. I'll be standing in front. Gilbert Martin."

When the blue police van pulled up to the house, two men and two women got out, dressed in the pressed khaki uniform of the

Israeli police.

"Would you tell us what happened exactly, Mr. Gilbert?" one of the policewomen asked.

As Gilbert explained, the taller, darker policeman translated for the other two.

"And this is the car, I'm sure of it," said Gilbert. "This man saw it pull up. And it turned around, you see, so that it would look as though it had come from the other direction."

"Well, let's go talk to the owner."

"Just a minute," said the tall policeman. "You say you are sure this is the same car."

"Yes."

"How are you sure?"

"Well, it's the only Volkswagen here."

"There are many white Volkswagens in Israel. Did you see the registration?"

"The what?"

"The registration. The number."

"Oh, you mean the license plate. No. It was too fast."

"Did you see any special marks on the car?"

"No."

"And you say the car came up this narrow road."

"That's right."

"It's in the wrong direction."

"I told you. It turned around."

"But you did not see it turn around."

"No. But this man did." Gilbert indicated the man whose phone he had used. "He's a witness."

"Okay. We shall see. Now let's talk to Mussa."

"Who's Mussa?"

"He lives here. He owns the car."

"You know him?"

"Yes. He is well-known."

"Mussa. Is that a Jewish name?" asked Gilbert.

"Mussa comes from Baghdad. His name is Arabic for Moses. He is like you a Jew. But a dark one. Like me. Eastern Jew. Sephardi. You understand me?"

Gilbert understood only that the distance between Iraq and Illinois was not easily reconciled.

As they went through the gate and up to the imposing house, one of the policewomen stayed behind to talk to the witness. Gilbert could see the man shake his head, lift his shoulders, and spread his arms in the Mediterranean gesture of individual bafflement before implacable and completely unreasonable reality.

The door was opened by a handsome man in his mid-sixties with a sun-crinkled face, thick black hair with a touch of white at the temples, and a white mustache drooped and shaped as Gilbert had seen among the Druse elders. Even dressed in dusty, sun-bleached clothes, the man exuded power. He welcomed the police into a small foyer where they all started talking rapidly in Hebrew.

Gilbert couldn't follow and wasn't really interested. He was looking beyond the discussion and into the house. A young man draped in gold chains sat on a white sofa with another young man and drank from a full glass of beer. They ignored the police completely, secure, Gilbert realized, in Mussa's ability to protect them.

"What's he saying?" Gilbert asked the policewoman who had spoken English to him. But she held up her thumb and two fingers pressed together as if balancing a marble. Gilbert knew enough Hebrew to know the gesture meant "just a moment." Then the policewoman who had been interrogating Gilbert's witness came in and started talking rapidly to the tall policeman who seemed to be in charge.

"What's going on? What's he saying?"

"He says there has been some mistake," said the policewoman.

"What mistake?"

"Mussa says his wife was driving the car. She was in the supermarket. The vegetables are here in the kitchen. Mussa says she came home a little time ago but she did not come up this narrow road. She came up the big road next to the fields. That's why the car is parked facing down the narrow road. Mussa says his sons have been here for an hour with him. Mussa says many cars come down the narrow road and drive away. The people come from somewhere else. They don't belong here. And there are many Volkswagens in Israel."

"But what about the man next door? That's not what he says."

"Ah, yes. This man thinks you maybe did not understand. He saw nothing."

"Nothing?"

The tall policeman was thanking Mussa and backing everyone out of the house as the two insouciant boys continued to neglect them.

"God damn it!" said Gilbert when they were all standing out on the road in the early evening. "Those boys did it. I know they did it. I don't care what anybody says."

"Yes. Of course," said the tall policeman. "Mussa protects his own."

"But if you know they did it, why don't you arrest them?"

"I have no facts. No evidence."

"What about the man next door? Can't you make him tell the truth?"

"He lives here. He is Mussa's neighbor. He must protect himself and his family."

"Damn it," said Gilbert. "I'm going to press charges anyway. I want to file a complaint. Let's settle the matter in court."

"You can do this. But you must talk to a lawyer first. Discuss the facts with him. Then if you want to make a complaint, come to the police station."

Gilbert had been in enough negotiations to know when he was being finessed.

"What's your name?" he asked.

"Avi."

"Avi, you say that Mussa is known to the police."

"Yes."

"What for?"

"Mussa does many things--even prostitution."

"Prostitution?"

"Yes. We will get him and his sons maybe one day. But not today."

"Prostitution? What kind of a job is that for a Jew?"

Avi looked at him with amusement.

"The girls are Jewish, too," he said.

"What!"

"Yes. It is a vicious business. And Mussa is a violent man. I do not want anyone hurt on such a small business of an orange. Talk to your lawyer. Tell him everything. But if you listen to what I tell you, you will forget about this. You will not win. You have not facts."

"But I have the will to win."

Avi looked at him.

"I can be ruthless," said Gilbert, remembering his triumphs in the boardroom.

"You are American, yes?"

"From Chicago," said Gilbert, smiling his broad American smile that set so many negotiators at ease.

They stood about in awkward silence.

"What's going on?" Gilbert asked.

"I can give you a tramp back to your house?"

"No, thank you. I'm walking for my health."

"Talk to your lawyer first," said Avi, getting into the police van beside the others. "Then if you want to make a complaint ...."

"Yes."

Gilbert walked home through the evening the way he had come--among the fields and houses, past the cemetery and the orchards.

He opened the security door with his key and rang for the elevator. He turned, by chance, to look out into the street, and, just before the door closed, he glimpsed a white Volkswagen. As the security door clicked shut, the elevator doors opened. He stepped inside quickly.

"Hello, dear. Did you have a nice walk? You've been gone a long time."

"No, I did not. I've been with the police."

"What happened? What did you do?"

"I didn't do anything. I was attacked."

"Attacked?"

"Some kids threw an orange at me out of a fast-moving car."

"Assault with a deadly orange, eh?"

"It's not funny, Loretta."

"I'm sorry, dear, but you seem to be fine. Did it hit you?"

"Hit me? It damn near killed me. Bowled me over. There I was, groveling in the dust, trying to catch my breath."

"But you're not hurt."

"No."

"Well, no harm done. Thank God for that."

"But I know who did it and that's why I called the police."

"Did the police arrest them?"

"No. Not enough evidence, they say."

"Then it's over. The Attack of the Flying Orange People! Disreputable Victim Disheveled! Perpetrators Unpunished. Call in Poirot!"

"It's not funny and it's not over."

"What do you mean it's not over? Are you going to press charges anyway?"

"Maybe. I want to talk to Wellman tonight and see what he says. It seems that the people who did this are part of a criminal family, into drugs and prostitution, and, you know, they're not Arabs. They're Jews."

"Criminals?"

"Yes. The police told me all about them."

"Jewish criminals? Here in Israel?"

"This certainly isn't Chicago."

She seemed to consider this.

"If you want some advice from a wife who loves you," she said, "you'll forget about it. Kids will be kids. No harm done. Perhaps your pride got a little dusty is all--but then, you're dressed for that, aren't you?"

"I can't wear a business suit when I go for a walk," he said.

"Will you change, please, before we go out?"

"I want to wear these clothes to the Wellmans."

"Victim of Assault by Ferocious Orange Throws Himself upon Mercy of Court in Original Rags."

"Very funny, Loretta."

"Have the Wellmans ever seen you in your original rags?"

"They're naïve," said Gilbert. "They think that people are the way they seem to be. I'm going to expose them to the dark underside of Israeli society."

"I hope at least that you're going to shower your dark underside before you go exposing it all over the place."

"I will," he said, moving off toward the bathroom.

"And change your clothes."

As Gilbert passed the door, the buzzer sounded. After an awkward moment he opened the door and looked out into the dark hallway.

"It's the intercom," she said.

He picked up the phone and listened. "Hello," he said.

No one answered.

"Kids," said Loretta.

But Gilbert pulled open the sliding windows in the living room and walked across the penthouse garden to look down into the street in front of their building.

Three white Volkswagens.

As he watched, he became aware of night replacing evening, of darkness whelming up from the east and falling everywhere. He closed the windows and pulled the sheers against the darkness, and, as he went past the front door on his way to the showers, he turned the key in the lock.

Testimony

So as I'm going out the door, I tell her I need the letters in English to Helena Rubinstein and the US Patent Office, letters in German to Vienna about the Bauer reparations money, and letters in Hebrew for the malpractice case against Cohen and the breach-of-promise case against Licht. And I tell her I need them by tomorrow.

She doesn't bat an eye.

And then I tell her, "if the Legal Adviser to the Prime Minister's Office calls back, I'll be at home until eight and at the Sheraton for the meeting of the British Friends of Israel after that."

And she says, "Yes, sir. See you tomorrow morning." Just like that! Can you imagine?

And then she gets up. I love it! She's six-foot-two in stockings and unfolds herself like some hyper-articulated giraffe. You've seen her. She's hung with more gold than most stores have to sell. You have no idea the impression she makes on clients.

No, no. I pay her what she's worth. I hired her for her brains, not her looks. I tell you--these modern Israeli girls. She's fluent in three languages and runs the office like a captain--which was actually her rank, by the way.

You haven't seen my new office yet, have you? Stop by when you're free. It's the most elegant building in Tel Aviv. Carrara marble and Czech crystal everywhere. And a Bokhara on the floor in the waiting room.

Yes, a fortune. But, you know, you get what you pay for, and style costs money.

The only complaint I have is that the building isn't quite finished. The foundation underneath where the parking should be is a shambles of trash and waste that seems to stretch back to the War of Independence. I have to park the Jaguar on the street!

Well, you can laugh, but it's always a shock coming from my office into Tel Aviv. It's a different world out there: the heat, the noise, the air gray with bus fumes. Anyway, I was at the corner of I-don't-know, Rashi, HaAvodah, one of those streets, and I see this really old lady with shocking red hair. She's standing in an aluminum walker, get this, with two plastic sacks of groceries at her feet. When the light changes, she reaches down first for one bag and then for the other. She stands up and grabs the walker. She lifts the walker off the curb. The light changes. She pulls the walker back up on the sidewalk and puts the groceries down.

It was the funniest thing I've ever seen. The groceries would grow roots through the pavement before she ever got organized enough to cross the street.

I came up to the corner, minding my own business, you know, just looking straight ahead as if she wasn't there.

"Help me," she says to me.

I looked at my watch. I wanted to indicate to her as clearly as I could that I've already done my *pro bono* for the month, but her eye never wavered. She had a face the color of rye bread speckled with caraway seeds, a lumpy nose with a sparkle about to drip from the end, and scarlet lips that clashed with her hair. She was a wonder. Her eye glittered with a tear or irritation or age or I-don't-know-what.

So I picked up the sacks. I mean, what else could I do?

I've never crossed a street more slowly. But when we got to the other side, she just kept going. I offered her the bags, but she didn't even see me. She simply assumed that I was going to schlep her groceries home for her. I was about to leave the bags on the sidewalk when she turned up this path beside an ancient, I mean an ancient building. Absolutely unreconstructed. The second-floor balcony had a stone balustrade supporting pillars with Moorish arches. You know what I mean? Alternating blue and white bricks? It must have been one of the original buildings of Tel Aviv, built for a single family in the '20s or '30s but now broken up into apartments with separate entrances and distinctive smells.

So she says to me, "Just a little farther, young man."

Ha! I don't remember when was the last time I was called "young man," do you? I followed her into a littered courtyard. Old kettles. Old bottles. A broken can. Up one step onto a patio and up another into just the sort of two-room, ground-floor apartment your grandmother lived in seventy-five years ago. Gray walls that used to be white and naked iron pipes rusted black at the joints. The room smelled of musty old furniture. An iron sink with a single, cold-water tap and a built-in corrugated drain--remember? Still see them every once in a while in Old Tel Aviv. And one of those two-burner gas stoves with a little pilot light burning in the middle like a synagogue.

So I crossed the room to put the groceries beside the sink. It was a mistake. The floor was tacky.

And then she says to me, "You will have some tea."

I told her I didn't want any tea but she didn't hear me, of course, and moved about the little kitchen without the walker, feeling her way from counter to refrigerator to sink to stove as though she were blind.

Then she says out of the blue, "Goldberg will come."

Goldberg? Who's this Goldberg? What's going on here? A committee meeting?

She was lighting this *yahrzeit* candle at the back of a narrow counter. And then she says to me, "They had to die, you know."

That was it. I had to get out of there.

But as I'm backing toward the door, I ask her, "Who had to die?"

"The boys. The two Eliahus."

"Who are they?"

"'Goldberg Watches,'" she says to me.

So that's when I said, "I really must go."

"Wait," she says. "I want to give you ...."

She starts feeling her way across the room to a bookcase in the corner, and she leaned on a rocking chair. I thought she was going to fall and I jumped to catch her.

"That chair is dangerous," I said.

And listen to what she says to me. "Yes," she says. "Ben Gurion sat there. The pig."

Before I could say a word, the door opened suddenly, and I turned to see.

"Goldberg," she says.

The man at the door was as thin as she was bulbous. Wispy hair. Watery blue eyes. Knobby hands with stiff, crooked fingers. But he was made of corded muscle and sprung steel. He had yellow, angled teeth, highly polished, and fallen inwards like a shark's. It wasn't his careful movements or shabby clothes which caught my eye and quashed the question I was about to ask about Ben Gurion. It was the gun in his belt. Now, you see people everywhere in Israel walking around with guns. But not someone in their mid-seventies carrying a pistol thrust into his waist-band. And what a pistol. Some massive weapon which I later learned was a Polish Nagan popular fifty years ago because it never jammed.

Shaking Goldberg's hand was like grasping a petrified branch. As we shook hands I noticed the gun was positioned to be drawn with his left.

So I said, "Nice to meet you, Mr. Goldberg. Thank you, lady, and goodbye."

I didn't really think that Goldberg would shoot me in the back
as I walked away, but the thought crossed my mind.

No, that's not the end of it. I went back to see her the next day.
I'll tell you why. It must have been when Goldberg entered that
she slipped a thin book into the side pocket of my briefcase. I
discovered it in the office the next morning. At first I couldn't
figure out what it was doing in my case--an old, really crumbly
student copy-book, a brown cover gray with age, and forty lined
pages. My present from the old lady. I opened it and saw poetry.
Poetry! God in heaven, was I to become the repository of her
juvenile longings, energized by hormones long dead and set in
verse? It was too grotesque.

Then one line caught my eye: "Quoth the Raven,
'Nevermore!'"--with the last word underlined in red crayon.
Unbelievable! Poe translated into Hebrew. I hadn't read Poe since
we studied English in--what was it?--tenth grade?

After I read a few lines, I knew it wasn't her stuff after all.

At the top of the page was written "Poems I Like." Poe's "The
Raven" was there and "Annabel Lee" and after these two was "V.
Jabotinsky." Yes, Jabotinsky! I suppose I once knew that
Jabotinsky was "literary," but I just don't connect the spiritual
mentor of Begin and the Irgun with Hebrew translations of Edgar
Allen Poe.

The book contained other poems. Tchernichovsky's *Pagan
Sonnets* and Bialik and Uri Zwi Greenberg, as well as other
translations into Hebrew of people I've never heard of.

Now you know I'm not much for poetry, but these poems were
all--how shall I say?--disturbing. They were all strong,
passionate--yes--but they were absolutist, extreme, yes, that's the
word. They were extreme. They allowed for no gray area where we
can work. The world they projected was either black or it was
white. And that was all. Listen, I remember a line or two of a poem
called "Hymn to the British Soldiers." It went something like this.

We are the men without name, without kin,
Who bleed for the land we were born to possess.
Earth! do not hide our blood!
Enrich, enrich the land and denounce
The rotting British heart which makes us kill.

I tried to imagine my secretary unfolding her gold-bespangled body in that world. It wouldn't fit. She might be someone's Annabel Lee, but no amount of sybaritic pleasure-seeking, no amount of gold or beer or partying would ever prepare her for the world defined in that notebook.

I didn't spend much time on it, mind you, maybe ten minutes, but it bothered me all day, and I wanted to return the book to the old lady. It seemed, I don't know, so out of place in Tel Aviv in the '90s.

Goldberg met me at the door, armed to the teeth.

I said, "Hello, Mr. Goldberg. I was here yesterday. Remember? I helped with the groceries."

But this guy just kept watching me.

"I've brought the notebook back," I said. I held it out for him to see. He let me in.

She was sitting at the tiny table. Two cups of tea steamed in the dusty sunlight that sort of angled through these tattered curtains. Then Goldberg closed the door behind me and I felt I was standing in shadow.

I showed her the notebook and told her I really couldn't accept it. "If you want your memories preserved," I said, "donate this to the Diaspora Museum or maybe Yad V'Shem."

That's exactly what I said. And she looks at me as though I'm crazy.

Maybe she didn't remember who I was, so I said, "The man who helped you yesterday."

"I know you," she said. And then she stands up and clears her throat with this horrid rasping sound and spits into the sink.

What's going on? So I turn to Goldberg and say, "What did I do?"

He looks at me--he's really scary--and says to me, "Do you really believe in those meaningless museums of Zionism?"

So I say, "What's the matter with Zionism?" It was like asking what's the matter with sunshine. You know what I mean?

Then she butts in and says, "We were building a new nation, not preserving an empty monument to dead culture."

I looked to Goldberg for some kind of . . . . and he says, "We lived here on the land. We had nothing to do with the dying communities of Europe and America. We were a Hebrew Liberation Movement interested in freeing our homeland from our British masters."

"British?"

"Of course the British," said Goldberg. "Who do you think the war was against?"

"Nazism. Totalitarianism."

"No," he said to me. "Europe was fighting the Nazis. We were fighting the Turks and the Brits. They were the same, don't you see? The point is that they were foreign."

"But the British are our friends," I said to Goldberg.

"Nazis," she said. "Worse than Nazis."

So again Goldberg finished her thought. He said, "If the *Sturma* and the *Patria* had been full of German soldiers, MacMichael would have interned them. But since the boats were full of Jews escaping from the concentration camps, the British sent them out to sea to die."

Well, no matter what the British had done in the past, to lump them with the Nazis as the common enemies of the Jews beggared believability. Okay, so there are a few Arabists in the Foreign Office. There are Arabists in every foreign office. We have to forgive and forget. Compromise and negotiate. That's the way the world works. How could I tell her that the British were our friends, and that the British Jews spread their largess like honey over the land?

Then she asked me if I knew the difference between the British and the Germans.

"Yes," I said. "The British won."

"But they never apologized," she said, wagging her finger at me. "They're still trying to kill the Jews."

Now really! I mean, I had to smile at her simplicity.

"Listen to the BBC," she said.

Well, I saw there was no point in talking to her about the way of the world and the generosity of the British, so I changed the subject. I asked her about Ben Gurion.

Goldberg snorted, and then he says to me, "Ben Gurion was a devious conniving piece of pedestrian offal. I wouldn't feed him to my dog if I had a dog. I spit on his memory."

And then she calls him "a collaborator." She says to me, "Hagannah thugs spied on the Irgun. And spied on us. Kidnapped us. Turned us over to the British. Ask 'Goldberg Watches,'" she says.

He looked at me with his steady eyes and crooked teeth. I didn't want to ask him anything.

"I was a watchmaker," he said, "so the British paid special attention to my hands." He showed me. The stiff fingers seemed to point in different directions.

So if they hated Ben Gurion so much, what was he doing there and why did he sit in that chair?

Then she explained that her mother was in school with Paula. And her mother didn't want her to rob banks or kill British policemen any more. So she asked Paula to send Ben Gurion around to tell her what the British do to girls in prison. Apparently he was most graphic, because when I asked her what she did after Ben Gurion talked to her, she said she went to Cairo.

Well, now. Evening was coming on. The part of the little room that held Ben Gurion's chair was in darkness. It was so quiet I could hear the memorial candle sputter and spit as the last bits of wick sucked up the molten wax on the bottom of the glass. I could see the light from the *yahrzeit* candle in her eyes.

She met the two Eliahus in Cairo. It was their notebook with the poems.

I was confused, so I asked who these Eliahu boys were.

She looked at me in that astonished madwoman's way of hers and says, "They killed Moyne."

Do you remember who Moyne was? Who remembers?

"Churchill's friend," she says. "A rich man," she says--and she said it with contempt as though wealth were irrelevant. And then she said, "Goodness. Goodness Beer."

Goldberg corrected her. It was "Guinness."

"I spit in his Guinness Beer," she says. "Murderer of the Jews."

Did you remember that Eliahu Hakim and Eliahu Bet Zouri assassinated Lord Moyne in Cairo? Goldberg was actually proud of it.

"What a rage there was!" he said.

They thought they had shaken the sleepy Jews around the world. Ben Gurion had to lick the British boots. And then the Egyptians hung the boys. Hakim was seventeen.

"Nevermore," she said.

The memorial candle sputtered in the corner. Even the thin March light was disappearing from the window.

"No one remembers," she said. "Two young boys executed a murderer and died for their country," she said. "I remember."

Well, I tried to commiserate, as one does, with mourners. I said they were too young to die. "Wasted lives," I said. "A few years later the state was founded."

But she would have none of it.

"They died for their country," she said. "Not for this state where the 'Rabbi' is prime minister."

Goldberg said, "We called Yizernitsky 'Rabbi' in those days. He calls himself Shamir now."

"Prime minister of the Arabs," she said. "And the crazy Jews who rob themselves by stealing from each other."

Again Goldberg translated: "The religious rob the government for their schools--some of which don't even exist. And the workers rob the government to support their corrupt union. The government prostitutes itself to every minor faction in order to rule--as if to rule meant only to decide where the money goes. Everybody wants the money. As if money were life."

"Money," she said with contempt, just as the memorial candle sputtered and died in the corner. The pilot light on the stove remained.

"This is not the state they died for," said Goldberg moving about in the dark. Suddenly the fluorescent light on the wall spit and hummed.

"It's the right country," she said. "But the wrong state."

But I was blinking against the sudden brightness.

Well, I had to go, so I left. I left the book, too. I wasn't the right person to keep it anyway. I should have straightened her out, explained the basis of western humanism to her--respect for all people before the law--all people, religious and non-religious, Arabs and Jews. But would it have been worth while? I don't know. She was clearly demented. And Goldberg would have been there with his shark's teeth and his massive revolver. I mean, what's the point of changing one old woman's opinion? No, she was a mad aberration, completely *non compos* with an insane legacy of absolutism better forgotten.

The next day I was back in my office where it's always temperate, winter or summer, and back with my stunning secretary, hung with gold and dressed in an electric green silk suit she picked up for a song in Bangkok. You know what? Sometimes, in the afternoons, she brings me lime sherbert in a Wedgwood bowl with a silver spoon from Gerrards.

Solange

All terminals are the same. It's a dull time in a dull place. I often don't know where I am anymore, nor do I care. Standing in line for security is tedious, except maybe in Madrid where everyone has a different story about how they got robbed. It's a national pastime there, a sport like soccer. Kids do it for kicks. Two guys on a Vespa.

I don't go into the towns much anymore. They're tedious too. The only thing that's important is how far they are from where I live. Rome and Vienna three hours. Zürich and Frankfurt four hours. Paris, London, Copenhagen five. New York eleven. That's how long I have to stay awake.

I sit in the last row of the middle cabin, center section, right-hand aisle. I watch the people bubbling through the aisles to find their seats and settle down. The large-mouthed knitting bag on my knees has all my airplane necessaries. A book on moral philosophy. A present for Meir. I knit on these trips to keep my fingers and wrists supple. Every member of my family has a sweater.

Take-off and landing are dangerous because people have to make decisions. Everything else is automatic. Everyone has a place. The pilots are in the cockpit, negotiating the plane's relationship to the earth. The stewards and stewardesses are strapped in. The passengers are bound in their seats. The aisles are empty.

Take-off is more dangerous for me. I start knitting as soon as I'm in the plane. It clears my mind. A kind of numbing stupor like a mantra suffuses my body so that only my hands are alive. Tiredness goes. Apprehensions vanish. Nothing remains except my moving hands on the dueling needles that slip silkily along each other, parrying and thrusting in a mindless game of endless repetition. Everything on automatic.

A man ten rows in front of me stands up against the upward slant of the plane and shouts "Allahu Akbar," his throat constricted with emotion and his voice thin and high and not very loud. He has a gun. Another man rises from mid-row on the right and stumbles toward the aisle. I don't see what he has.

I do what I do best. Crouching in the aisle, knees bent, fists overlapped on the grip of my target pistol, arms locked. Two seconds. Too much flesh and bone protecting his heart from this angle. I put two bullets under his ear at the base of his skull. Three seconds. The other man stands in the aisle looking for his friend. Three-quarter front view. I put a bullet through his eye. Four seconds.

The gun is back in the knitting bag and I am on my way to disappearing. There had been little sound from the muffled muzzle, no smoke.

"What the hell was that?"

"Nothing," I say. "We're doing a run-through for a movie."

I slip my arm through the large plastic rounds of the knitting bag and go to see what I've done, but the steward and a stewardess have already covered him with a blanket and begun to drag him forward.

Most people didn't see or hear anything. One of the hysterics is calmed by the steward and moved to first class. The plane buzzes with talk of danger past but doesn't waver. The rest of the trip is uneventful.

Later I saw a hole where the eye had been and scrambled

brains within it. No exit. The other's face is mottled and shredded where some of the bullet fragments came through. But the two entry holes were within three centimeters of each other. Quite acceptable at twelve meters.

There had been a third person, a woman, in the cabin behind me, but Elisheva brought her down with one shot at very close range. There were no others.

2.

All debriefings are the same. When nothing happens, which is just about all the time, we file a piece of paper and go home. But when something happens, it's not so easy. I have to go over the events six or seven times or eight times or ten times and almost always to the same people. Avi, the commander of my unit; the chief of aircraft security; the duty-officer at Ben Gurion; a representative from the foreign ministry and another from Shin Bet; and the chief of security in foreign airports.

It should take twenty minutes. There's not much to tell. But with so many officers, all of about the same rank, there's no one in charge so everyone talks at the same time and it takes hours.

"Nice shooting, Solange."

"Yeah, nice shooting."

"Thank…"

"Why did you shoot the man on the left first?"

"He had the gun. The other one was not quite on his feet. I'm more confident shooting to the left."

"What was he doing with the gun?"

"Waving it."

"Nice shooting, Solange."

"Did he say anything?"

"He said that God was great."

"Did he grab anyone?"

"What did it look like he was going to do?"

"Did you consider that he might be wired?"

"How did you know he didn't have explosives on his body?"

"Did you know he had a grenade?"

"No, I saw a gun."

"No, no. I mean the other guy."

"Nice shooting, Solange."

"I didn't see what he had. Both hands were busy getting him balanced and on his feet in the aisle. I didn't see a weapon."

"He had a grenade in his pocket."

"I didn't see a grenade."

"He picked it up on the plane. A cleaner planted it."

"You're kidding," Shin Bet said.

"No. Passenger security was good, but they got to this cleaner and convinced him to plant the grenade in the Kleenex compartment of the toilet."

"That's where the gun was, too."

"What did the girl have?"

"You won't believe this. A plastic gun. Graphite-reinforced, polymer-plastic taped to her calf. The metal scanner didn't pick it up."

"Listen, the Japanese are making automobile engines out of the stuff. And there's not much difference between a pressurized gas explosion and a gunpowder explosion."

"Shut up, you guys. Let's get back to this."

"So what did you do then, Solange?"

"When?"

"Nice shooting, Solange."

Finally they let me sleep. Or rather, they would have let me sleep.

"Go to sleep, Solange," they say as they file out of the room.

"Nice shooting."

And everyone leaves except the psychiatrist. Psychiatrists are all alike. They have a cloying timbre to their voice. They like to do good.

"You killed a man tonight."

"Two."

"Two. How are you going to deal with this?"

"I'm going to sleep now."

"That's good. That's one way of letting your mind heal. Because when you sleep, you dream. Tell me about your dreams."

"I have no dreams."

"Everybody dreams."

"I don't."

"What did you do after you shot that terrorist on the ground in Copenhagen four years ago?"

"I went to sleep."

"And you didn't dream then, either?"

"I have no dreams."

And then he prescribes the obvious: a five-kilometer run every day for a week and return to firearms practice.

"You have to push your body, Solange, push it hard. All the bad effects of killing that man will come out of your body in sweat."

"I run five-k every day. I ran this morning. I'll run again tomorrow morning. I run every morning."

"And get back to the shooting range. You have to feel the gun again. You have to hear it and smell it."

"I'm on the firing range almost every day for an hour. It sharpens the eye."

"You have to work through the natural feelings of guilt and remorse in order to live with the experience of killing a person."

"I have no trouble killing people who are interested in killing me."

"But you will."

"But I don't."

He looks at me with warm brown eyes. Standard issue for psychiatrists.

"Good night, Solange."

I tip over on the army cot and close my eyes.

"Nice shooting," he says as he turns out the light.

3.

My mother is sitting on the couch with Louise from upstairs. From the door to the couch is five meters.

"Solange, dear. Give your mother a hug and say 'hello' to Louise."

"'Lo, Louise."

"Hello, Solange."

"I'm so glad to see you, Solange. Give me a kiss. Are you hungry? Do you want something to eat? You look tired."

"No, I'm fine. I want to take a shower first of all. I didn't get to shower before I left the base."

"Where were you this time?"

"'At a base somewhere in Israel'."

"Isn't she terrible, Louise? That's all she ever tells us. Her own parents."

"And if I were to say 'The Corners' or 'Four Trees' or '631' would you know any more?"

"What do you do in the army, Solange?"

"They keep moving her around from place to place, Louise. Sometimes she comes home for the weekend, sometimes not. I never know when to expect her. She never tells her mother anything."

"I'm just a job-nik."

"And it's not even a real job, Louise. Sometimes she's home four-five days in a row. I mean, what sort of a job is that? How important can it be? She seems to spend all her time knitting. She doesn't even get to wear a uniform."

"Do you like what you do in the army, Solange?"

"Yes. I'm learning skills I can put to good use in the world when I get out."

"I mean, really, Louise, how can the neighbors tell that I have a child in the army if they don't see a uniform hanging out to dry? When Noach is called up for reserve duty, the laundry-lines are crowded with army green. What do I get from Solange? Nothing."

"What are you going to do when you get out of the army? Are you going to go to the university?"

"University! Louise, bite your tongue. Studying is not what Solange does best. Don't let Noach hear you. Noach doesn't believe girls should go to the university. He doesn't think they belong in the army either. Always getting in the way, he says."

"No, I think I'll go on a trip."

"That's what they all do when they get out of the army, you know, Louise. Traveling, traveling. Got to get out. It's like a sickness. You know the Sharabachs in four? Cute woman with curly hair from Morocco? Her oldest son, Motti, signed on three extra years and rose to be a captain and when he got out, he went traveling. Well, he was riding a bus in the middle of nowhere Peru when the bus went over the mountain. Just like that. Six years in the army without a scratch, and he dies in Peru. It really makes you think."

"Are you interested in traveling to South America, Solange?"

"No."

"She's so vague, this child of mine. Solange, dear. Take your knitting out of the living room, please. We have a guest."

All apartments are pretty much alike. The number of rooms may differ but the basic organization is the same. Once an architect gets an idea for an apartment, that's all he can see. He has to keep the plumbing lined up.

We have mirror-image bedrooms on both sides of the hallway.

Mine is the last on the left facing the back. The view from my window is across ten meters of driveway to the apartment house behind. Cars below. Sun-collectors for hot water on the roof above. That's about as much open space as I can take. I can look outside so long as it's not my responsibility and I don't have to deal with it. I don't like being out of doors. The vistas are too open, the distances too great. Too much wind and glare. Too many variables. I'm an indoor person. Clearly defined, internal space. Subdued light. No sudden gusts. A uniform color that washes away to unobtrusive background and brings out the shine in the darkest eye.

My piano is black. I used to play the piano before I took up knitting. My brothers write their names in the dust on the closed lid.

I like to sleep in the black. Even on the hottest nights, I close the blinds and close the windows and close the curtains. The bedrooms facing the street always let in some light.

In summer, the showers are never cold enough, the night never black.

4.

I awake and look about. The other students are filing out of the room. Seven meters away, Dr. Zissenwine is talking to three students at the front of the room. Jewish Moral Philosophy from the Rashi to the Rambam. The green board behind him provides a perfectly acceptable self-effacing background.

As I gather my books and start for the door, he catches my eye.

"Solange."

"Yes ...?"

"Where are you going?"

"I beg your pardon?"

"I asked you to stay after class for a moment."

He looks at me.

"You didn't hear me, did you?"

I look him in the eye.

"That's what I want to talk to you about," he says.

So I wait and follow him to his office on the lee side of the building where the light is less bright. A dull undersea room with green-yellow light darkening toward late afternoon. A bathysphere lined with books.

"You seem to have a problem, Solange, and one of my jobs is to provide some guidance for the perplexed." He smiles. It's a joke. A literary allusion.

"I don't have a problem."

"Something seems to be putting you to sleep whenever you come into my class--which, I admit, isn't too often. If it's not your problem, then maybe it's mine. Let's see. Am I boring you? Fuzzy sentences? Monotonous voice?"

"No. You're a very interesting lecturer."

"Well, maybe it's the material? Perhaps the subtle distinctions in Maimonides' responsa to Rashi put you to sleep."

"No, I understand all that."

"The class doesn't meet too late in the afternoon for you? People usually fall asleep after lunch, between two and four."

"No, it's not that."

"Well, if it's not me and not the material and not the time of day ...."

"No."

"So then the problem is yours and not mine after all."

We look at each other in that earnest way that teachers and students do when they don't see eye to eye on things.

"Look, Solange, you come to my class irregularly. You fall asleep in the back row. You never contribute anything to the class. Your written work, when you hand it in, is good but not polished and not enough. Everything you do is incomplete. You might want to reconsider your commitment to a university degree."

"Dr. Zissenwine, a degree is really important to me."

"Then why do you sleep in my class?"

"I'm tired. I ... I've been up all night. I fly."

"What?"

"I work for El Al. I usually arrive here in mid-morning, after being on my feet all night, and by the time we clear the paper-work and I get over here from the airport, I haven't slept for twenty-two hours and the first chance I have to sit down is in your class."

"You're a stewardess?"

"Yes. And the only class I can take this semester is yours because it meets late in the afternoon on days when I'm generally not scheduled to fly."

"How can you do this? How can you possibly do justice to a full-time job with irregular hours and go to the university at the same time? And I suppose you're married?"

"Yes. It takes a lot of time."

"I understand."

I watch him thinking of ways to be helpful. One of the limitations of western philosophy is the need to reach out and understand others. Humanists have a crippling need to be helpful, to understand the "thou." It's a waste of time from Plato to Aristotle, from Augustine to Wittgenstein. But it was appropriate for where we were, beneath the sea, in a bathysphere filled with books, all designed to help us understand the fish.

5.

Sometimes I sleep with Meir. Career Army. Commander of Paratroops. It's not exactly love and it's not exactly need. It's like the knitting, but more somber. Sometimes his amber eye fills my internal space with millions of wriggling proto-souls which I systematically catch and kill.

Meir sincerely believes that it is possible to throw oneself out of an airplane at twelve-thousand feet and survive. He has told me what it is to fall through limitless light toward a distant and blurry earth while a ferocious wind screams in your ear and tears at your clothes and rams up your nose and mouth until the chute opens and the harness jerks your body upright like a buoy in a storm and what it's like to see a hundred miles of the earth's surface while you're plummeting toward earth at the same time that you're being jerked aloft by crotch straps and body bindings.

"Don't," I say. "Don't."

We live in a small apartment on the fourth floor of a building in the Florentine quarter of Tel Aviv. We knocked out all the internal walls to make one large room almost nine meters square. With the louvered blinds opened wide, what used to be the living room window gives Meir an unobstructed view of the sky, the jumbled rooftops of Tel Aviv, and the distant sea. I sit with my back to the window. It seems to satisfy both of us.

"Nice shooting, Solange," he says. "I just heard about it this morning."

"I'm getting out," I say.

"When?"

"Three months."

"Sign on for another tour."

"It's not that easy."

"Why not? You've already got six years invested. Sign on. Your salary will increase. You'll get a larger mortgage. They'll pay for graduate school. You might even get a car and driver."

"It's not that, Meir."

"Then what's the problem?"

I turn the wine glass in my hand.

"I just don't see what another year or two or ten in the army is going to do for my life. I know what I do. I know what I'm good at. Three more years in the army is only more of the same, not better."

"But you'll advance. They'll put you in charge of a security section somewhere, maybe an embassy, or give you Avi's job. There are limitless possibilities in the army."

"And after the army?"

"After the army is like after life, Solange. Who knows what it is?"

"Another year in the army is not going to make me any better prepared for life than I am right now."

"And what's that?"

"I shoot straight and fast. I judge distances and possibilities. I disappear in crowds. I have an eye for an eye."

"Excellent credentials. Stockbroker, I think. Or kindergarten teacher."

"I used to have other skills."

"You still do."

"I was thinking of music."

"I was thinking of bed."

It is an argument that goes nowhere. An indeterminate assault against an impregnable opinion.

6.

Spring is hard for me. A kind of depressing exuberance infuses the world. Trees stand up straighter and lose their crisp shape in pale, furry green. Sunlight lasts longer. Worst of all, the orange blossoms fill the air with a stench so cloying that I gag and choke. My lungs hurt. My eyes itch. A film of tears clouds my vision. I lose my eye.

That's when I like to close myself into an air-filtered box with measurable meterage and subdued light. Airplanes are good. Movie theaters are good. My room in my parents' house or my apartment, when Meir isn't there to open windows, is good.

That's why I like to fly. The rules are perfectly clear. I sit. I knit. I stay awake. If the trip is uneventful, I file a short report and go to sleep. If there is trouble, I solve it.

It's the world outside the plane that causes all the problems. Meir and windows and free-falling. Psychiatrists who treat the incurable with the ineffectual. Proud parents. Helpful teachers who teach how to understand stockbrokers and other children.

I just don't see it.

Which is why, in a dark, air-conditioned room, with my target pistol in my fist, I find my eye.

Help

With rue my heart is laden
For golden friends I had

Tirtzah came from the house into the bright garden. The lawn was choked with birds leaping in a frenzy of feeding upon the green worms that dangled on silver filaments from the trees. Up they leaped: up. Up they leaped: up.

She tried to be still while the birds gorged, but the cats were with her. Suddenly the birds were gone in a flurry of flutter beneath the trees, out of the shadow and across the sun into the orchard beyond the lane.

The cats stared up at her, weaving between her feet, circling for position. She set down the bowl of chicken flesh saved from the dinner and separated from bone. The cats struck at the bowl and hunkered down to feed.

Tirtzah came down the stairs and across the filament-infested yard. Her skirt and hair grew rich in worms. She brushed them down as the gorgeous garden called to her in oranges and yellows and gold.

She spread last night's coffee grounds beneath the rose bushes and turned them into the soil with a trowel. She examined the crumbly underdirt for wire-worms, then mounded it carefully around the stems. She spread dry tea leaves over the roots of asparagus ferns opening arthritic fronds of new growth. She nipped dead leaves from geraniums. She inspected the dahlias for crowds of aphids. The sweet buds of ripening figs were already protected by blue plastic bags.

As she turned to go into the house, Tirtzah saw that worms, repelling from the trees, had already fallen into the cat food.

"Don't go today," he said from the porch, looking at her.

"How's your hand?"

"Oh, much better." Ezra held up the hand which she had expertly bandaged and opened and closed his fist upon air. "You did a good job."

"Drive carefully."

"You're going then?"

"She needs me, Ezzi."

"She doesn't even know you're there."

"She needs me every day."

"I need you here," Ezra said as he gathered her into his arms. "Come."

His briefcase knocked against the small of her back as she allowed herself to be gathered.

"Come to me, Tirtzah," she had said, folding the frail girl into her smelly skirts, her massive meaty arms falling about her as light and as warm as a feather comforter. "There, there," she said, "shhhhhh, shhhhh, my darling, my baby," rocking as the wind rocks, mourning as the doves mourn in the dirty dovecote behind the house. "I need you, my sweetheart, my darling, baby girl. Now dry your tears and take this bowl and help me snap the beans. We'll find your Baba before the sun goes down or we'll make you another tonight."

"I need you," Ezra said, "happy and whole, and you always come back destroyed."

2.

For many a rose-lipt maiden
And many a lightfoot lad.

For a moment, Tirtzah couldn't tell if anyone was there. The six beds were all in place, the various drips and monitors in silent attendance, but the beds were rumpled, empty. They had been hastily evacuated, the covers thrown back awry and twisted into grotesque shapes of abandonment and loss as if the alarm had shrilled and everyone had made a hasty breathless awkward dash for the shelter.

Only then did she see the tiny white heads upon pillows, the tiny faces that seemed to be made of cruelly crumpled paper badly shaped into balls of crushed discard topped by wisps of silver filament through which the skull gleamed. Tiny faces. Tiny, tiny faces, with tiny black eyes awash in some blue or yellow liquid. And with a dangerous dark hole where the mouth used to be.

"Come away, Tirtzah. Be careful. Don't fall in."

"But I forgot to say goodbye."

"What?"

"When I went to school. Today. This morning. I forgot to say goodbye when I went to school this morning."

"He can't hear you now, Tirtzah."

"I forgot to say...."

"Tirtzah, come away."

She found her mother there, her tiny face left to lie upon a pillow and dwarfed by twisted mounds of rumpled blanket. She leaned close to the dark hole and turned her ear to listen for the mourn of the sweet doves, rhythmic and warm. She saw her mother's delicate ear, the wrinkled lobe pierced but empty for the first time in eighty years. The triple-tiered golden hoops strung with beads were gone. She was becoming someone Tirtzah could no longer identify.

Tirtzah searched beneath the blankets for her mother's melted body. She found it and straightened it. Who was this starved ghost of wobbly skin loosely attached to sticks? She neatened the blankets and was about to lift her mother's head to puff the pillow when she saw the green worm on the lobe of her mother's ear. She picked it off gently before it disappeared within. She carried it out to the balcony at the end of the room and set it in the sun on the sill.

When she returned, her mother's head had fallen over in her direction. The eyes were open and the dark hole twisted wryly into what must have been a smile. She lifted her arm to Tirtzah, the flesh wagging.

Tirtzah changed her mother's diaper, wiping the flaccid, wrinkled flesh with tissue dampened in Lazar's Paste. While she examined the greenish stain for the tiny wriggle of pinworms and parasites, her mother stared at the ceiling. There was only care now; there was no healing to be done. So long as Tirtzah did their work, the nurses didn't disturb her. There were few eager nurses among the abandoned and the waiting.

Tirtzah washed her hands and then sat beside the bed. She held her mother's crumpled fist. She talked to her, though she could never know what her mother heard or remembered, whether her mother was asleep or resting with her eyes closed. Only the breathing told Tirtzah her mother was alive. Sometimes the fist moved.

When lunch came, Tirtzah fed her. Always messy. Never successful. Completely irrelevant since whatever nourishment kept her alive dripped into her arm from a bottle. As Tirtzah rose to leave, her mother's arm slipped like a pale gray tape-worm from beneath the blanket. She turned her delicate wrist upwards, the stringy sinews taut and the veins starkly blue and alive within the translucent skin. Slowly the tiny fist opened. And there, from the last time she was lucid, lay a crumpled slip of paper long since molded to the inside of her palm.

Tirtzah took the note and carefully opened it. Two lines written in block capitals, each leaning in a different direction.

"HELP ... ME ... PLEA ...."

Her throat tightened in terror, but she leaned over and wiped the wet from her mother's face.

3.

By brooks too broad for leaping

The flowers in the pot beside the door to Dr. Shalev's house were dead. Too much water. Too much of the wrong care. The leaves were brown and the roots rotted. A black slug lay in the slick earth of the container. She turned away and rang the bell. But the indoor plants were no better, and the complicated wicker birdcage that hung in the stairwell was empty.

She sat on the tatty sofa in the hallway outside the receiving room. On the wall before her were the Hippocratic Oath, framed in brushed aluminum, and "Therefore, choose life. Deuteronomy 30:19" worked in faded needlepoint by someone's European grandmother.

Dr. Shalev looked up from his messy desk to smile at her.

"Yes, Tirtzah, what can I do for you?"

"I'm not sleeping well, Yair."

"Well, I'm not surprised. With two boys in Lebanon and the twins about to graduate. It's a wonder you sleep at all. But Tova should be a great source of joy for you. How is she?

"Yes."

"Whenever she comes here, she is always so cheerful. Such a personality. So full of life and energy. One has to be young ...."

"You're too young, Tirtzah. I was younger than you and look

at me now. A fat widow who bore nine children. Two lost in the
wars and three in childhood. Only four left, my darling, my helper.
Don't leave me now when I need you most. Who will help cook?
Who will help with the garden?"

"She must be a great help to you."

"She can't help me sleep, Yair."

"No, no. Of course not. Perhaps a sedative. Numbon is good.
It's like Valium."

"Can we try something like Bondormin?"

"Well, I prefer to start with something milder."

"I prefer to start with something effective."

"Okay, Tirtzah. Bondormin is it, then. You'll sleep like a baby.
Ten pills should do for a start."

"Yes. That should do it."

"Don't take them all at once!" he laughed.

4.

The lightfoot boys are laid

The puppies tumbled and ran, stopped and tumbled about each
other and ran again. They stopped and hunted and leaped and
chewed each other's ears and tumbled and ran. Cats watched them
with disdain.

A boy and a girl from the moshav at the end of town rode
down the street on horses brown as chocolate, round as apples,
stepping high, their massive meaty haunches moving. Their iron
hooves clattered on the asphalt as they skittered sideways in their
energy and pride. The riders were as light as eiderdown on the bare
brown backs.

Pink nose and whiskers beneath the bushes. A rat--perhaps a
baby 'possum or only a field mouse--appeared cautiously in the
shadows that separated the garden from the field. The cats

stiffened. Josh and Shua slipped off the porch and into the holly beside the house, but the mole or whatever it was disappeared.

Time to go.

"Where are you going?"

When she didn't answer, he said, "You're not going to the hospital now."

"Ezzi ...."

"This is a sickness, Tirtzah."

She gave him a smile so down-daunted and wan that he abandoned his annoyance and brought her into his arms again.

"This is a sickness, Tirtzah, it really is," he said softly into her hair.

"There's some cold chicken in the 'frige and artichoke salad. Cut a tomato."

"I won't die," he said.

She felt him pulling gently at her hair and looked up.

"Inch-worm," he said as it squooshed between his fingers. "I'll be glad when it's over."

She looked at him.

"The birds can't eat them fast enough," he laughed. "And they eat everything."

They eat everything, she thought.

"So when will you be back?" Ezra asked.

"Don't know. Later. Sometime."

"Well, if you're not back, I'll tape *thirty-something* for you, okay? We'll watch it when you come back. Won't that be fun?"

5.

The rose-lipt girls are sleeping

Tirtzah changed her mother's diaper again, and out of habit looked at the slender, green-brown stain. She brought it under the light. There they were. Tiny. White. No more than half a centimeter. Twisting. Lifting out of the mess. She crushed the diaper and threw it away.

She powdered the pills and dissolved them in a small glass of water. She gently lifted her mother's head and helped her sip, her own mouth pursed as though the air she was sucking were the milky water itself.

"Drink this, Tirtzah, my darling. Drink this. It's good for you. It will make the pain go away. It will make the baby come. There, there, my baby, my darling. There, there. Drink. Yes. That's a good girl. There's a new life coming. A new life."

There was one other sentient person in the room, but he left in time to be home for the evening news. A night nurse came by and turned off the overhead lights. She wouldn't return until morning.

Tirtzah sat in the semi-darkness made by the spill of light from the hall and the moon in the window. She listened to the night noises surrounding her, the choke and cough and sniff, the murmuring, muttering, grumbling of words in many languages, the memories of the dead in the dreams of the dying.

Only her mother breathed evenly, deep now and evenly. Without pain. Without memory. Without feeling. Without hope.

Tirtzah took from her purse the brilliant blue plastic bag that preserved the budding figs from worms. She softly lifted and gently laid her mother's head within. She drew the strings. She mounded the covers carefully about her mother's face so the plastic would not be seen from the doorway. She took her mother's tiny fist in hers. She waited. The blue bag puffed and condensed, puffed and condensed.

6.

In fields where roses fade.
--A. E. Housman

The sun was bright. The golden garden called to her.

"My mother died last night," she said.

"O, Tirtzah, I'm so sorry." He took her unresisting body into his arms. He gave her a squeeze. And a pat. He held her at arm's length and looked at her. He brought her back into his arms. He patted her on the back.

"Are you all right?" he asked, letting her go. "It seems to me you've been grieving for so long already. It must be a relief to have reached a conclusion."

"The issue was never in doubt," she said.

"No, no. Of course not. But, I mean, it's over now. You don't have to go to the hospital every day."

"Come to me, Tirtzah."

"You can get back to your regular life. I need you and the twins need you."

"I need you, Tirtzah."

"As big as they are, you know, the twins miss you dreadfully. Tova especially. Over the past two months, you just haven't been here for her. She's been mourning the loss of you for as long as you've been grieving for your mother. But now that she's gone, you can come back to her.

"Come back, Tirtzah. Don't leave me."

"You can be here when Itay and Oded come home from the army. We can have a big cook-out again. The six of us. Chicken barbecued on the grill. Cole-slaw. Your great orange and melon salad with strawberries. Baked potatoes swimming in butter. We can even invite some people over again."

"Be careful, Tirtzah."

"You're free from her and the hospital. You never have to go back there again."

It didn't seem to warm her. Nothing seemed to warm her, frozen in her grief.

"Come with me, Tirtzah."

"And she's free, too," he continued, trying again. "Yes. She's free now from all the busy cares of this life."

He smiled reassuringly.

"They are busy with me, Tirtzah. I feel them turning in my intestines. Soon the little stain I have to feed them will be gone. And then they will turn upon the tissue in my bowels. I feel their tiny teeth, Tirtzah. They are coming in the blood. My meat is alive with them. They are falling in the dark hole and eating where my teeth ate. They are busy with my tongue, Tirtzah, I see them in my eyes. Help me, Tirtzah. HELP ME PLEA ...."

Test

"On Sunday, then," he said, puffing himself up to his full height, like the frog in the fable, the fluorescent light shining off his naked head and glinting from his bifocals, "you'll have a test covering all the material on the syllabus, including everything I've assigned that you have read and everything I've assigned that you haven't read."

He smirked as though he had made a joke.

"The problems are really easy to solve. All you need to know are Alan Turing's seminal work on morphogenesis as well as McCulloch and Pitts and the more recent von Neumann and Kleene on the neurophysiological aspect of automata theory. Pay special attention to the problems interconnecting elementary automata of the disjunctive, conjunctive, and negative types, as well as the probabilistic questions posed by Wiener when immersing a Turing machine in a random environment."

He smiled. He was having a good time.

"Just the sort of thing to separate all you sheep from all you goats, the *shin* speakers from the *sin* speakers. Those who survive can have their assistantships renewed," he joked.

Esti looked at the syllabus and rolled her eyes toward the ceiling.

"If you've been doing the work, you need only review. If you haven't been doing the work--well, that's what I want to find out, isn't it? And please, no excuses. I've heard them all. Don't be suddenly taken to hospital for an emergency operation unless you can bring a signed report from the entire medical team. Don't be in auto accidents unless you have a full police report with insurance estimates of the damage. Don't let anyone die in your family. Some students have grandmothers who die two or three times a year." He smirked again at his cleverness. "Just be here and be ready to push and pop from the stack. Bring books, notes, pencils, and brains. Any questions? That's all."

Esti gathered her belongings and held them tight to her chest.

Sigi whispered to her: "What a schmuck."

"I don't know what I'm going to do."

"Come have a coffee with us."

"No, I can't," said Esti. "I'm running the computer lab today and fielding software problems. Then I've got to get home and then to work. Dov's home early today, and I can't ask Arik to baby-sit."

"Why not?"

"It's a little sticky right now."

2.

--disjunctive

Buses never arrive on time. She sheltered in the bus stop against the brisk wind that rushed under the plastic walls and whipped around her ankles. She stamped her feet to a song in her head to keep warm. The rain came before the bus but she hadn't brought an umbrella. She was equally unprepared when the bus finally did arrive and gave the driver a fifty-shekel note for a six-shekel-fifty bus ride.

"This is Egged, lady, not Bank Leumi."

She endured his brown scowls in silence. As she clung to the bar behind the driver's seat and waited for her change, people pushed roughly around her, their winter fur making them take up more space than expected. The rain had fully arrived by the time the bus reached her stop, and the driver, in vicious reprisal, stopped too far for her to leap onto the curb. She stepped into the stream of water, cold in her shoe, cold around her ankle, and quickly got out of the way as the rear wheels of the bus splashed through the water in the gutter.

As she approached her apartment, she saw the luggage rack on Arik's car covered with a plastic sheet and the back seat piled with clothes.

"Oh," she said.

The door to the apartment was open. Arik was putting the last of his cassette tapes and CDs into his waste-paper basket in the center of the living room.

"Arik."

"No," he said. "I can't and I won't. We've had this conversation a thousand times. It was always going to be a trial arrangement. Well, the trial is over, Esti. It didn't work. We both have to face that."

Her right foot squooshed in her shoe. Her coat dripped on the rug. The rain on her face was salty.

"Weren't you even going to say 'good-bye'?"

"Good-bye," he said as he lifted the basket and went out the door.

She was sitting on the sofa not quite dry and completely alone in the cold apartment when Dov came home. He dropped his back-pack of books inside the door and looked around.

"Hey," he said. "What's going on?"

"Come to your mother," she said as she gathered him, resisting, into her arms.

"What is it?" he said, twisting.

"Arik won't be living with us anymore," she said.

"Oh," and as she hugged him to her, he went limp.

"Daddy fell in Lebanon," she crooned, "Lebanon, Lebanon / Daddy fell in Lebanon / Ten--no, it's eleven now, isn't it?--Eleven years ago."

She buried her face in his hair that curled the way his father's did.

"Dov was a little baby, then / Baby then, baby then." She held him to her, his tough body bristling under his coat.

"Dov was a little baby then, / But he's a big boy now."

"What's for lunch?" said Dov, twisting out of her arms.

3.

--conjunctive

She worked in a falafel stand until eleven o'clock three nights a week. She didn't mind the work though she hated the smell. The work was easy since she had only to stuff falafel into a pita and hand it to customers who helped themselves. She kept the bowls of condiments filled. Peppers and onions, hot and red, sprinkled with paprika. Baby eggplant pickled purple, cut in half, awash in sauce--about the size and color of an unfortunate fetus. Rumanian eggplant slightly piquant. Sharp, hot, Turkish salad. Dull green pickles; shiny bell peppers. Muddy yellow mustard sauce and beige tehina. Pickled cauliflower like shards of shattered brain. French fries the color of desert dust. And hot balls of falafel, starkly brown in many shades.

It was the stench of the oil in which she prepared the falafel and the French fries that made her queasy. Against the stained back wall, old black vats of cooking oil seethed beneath wire baskets hanging from the rack. All too often, she would spill French fries from the stiff plastic freezer-bag into the wire basket and lower them into the oil that screamed and sputtered and filled the air with white oily steam that slicked upon her skin and hung in her clothes and hung in her hair which, even after she washed it, smelled like a freshly mopped hospital corridor.

At a quarter to eleven the owner drove up in his Volvo 940 to clear out the cash register, put away the food, and lock up the stall.

"Mira tells me you were late again today, Esti."

"I'm sorry, Mr. Mugrabi. It was a personal problem."

"Look, Esti, we all have personal problems. Mira has personal problems. She has to go home to feed her children. I have personal problems. Yes, even me. You think it's easy to pay taxes and VAT and insurance every month? Everybody has personal problems. That's no excuse for being late for work."

There was nothing to say.

"I like you," he said. "I watch you. You do good work. You don't cheat on the cash register. You're an honest girl. So, okay, sometimes you read books."

He pointed at the open book on the counter, pages of formula speckled with micro-drops of ambient oil.

"Do I complain? No. I know you're pushing. But let me tell you, Esti, there's a limit. We all have responsibilities. We all have to meet them. That's called 'civilization.' You have an obligation to be here from four in the afternoon until eleven at night. That's your duty three evenings a week, and you either have to meet that obligation or look for another job. I can't jeopardize my whole business because you have personal problems."

They put the bowls into the refrigerated case to appear the next day, old mixed with fresh. The few greasy French fries and desiccated falafel balls that remained, he dumped into the garbage. While he pulled in the tables, she stacked the blue plastic chairs and prepared to mop the floors. He paid her in cash for the week's work, and she caught the last number 4 bus, racketing home in dismal light through the black streets of Tel Aviv.

The apartment was only slightly warmer than the bus. Anita, the high-school girl who sat with Dov three nights a week, had turned the electric heater on to take the edge off the chill. Esti wanted a shower; she needed a shower. The red light glowing high on the wall indicated that Anita had turned on the hot-water heater before she made love to her boyfriend on Esti's bed. The covers were always disheveled, and more than once Esti was surprised by damp spots when she slipped down between the sheets. Esti had to let her get away with everything.

Esti looked into Dov's room, little more than a converted closet. His blankets were thrown back; he was not in his bed. The light in the bathroom was on. She listened at the door for bathroom sounds. She tapped at the door.

"Dov? Hi, baby. It's mommy."

No sound.

"Dov? Are you all right?"

She leaned on the door which opened with difficulty. First she saw the words "I am shit" smeared on the wall and then she saw the naked boy asleep on the cold floor and then she saw the stark brown excrement smeared on his body and then she saw the bright blood oozing up around the knife sticking impossibly out of his thigh.

4.

--and negative

"Your father couldn't come," said her mother. "Someone had to watch the shop. Two of the Arab workers didn't come in again. A Russian family rented the apartment upstairs. He couldn't get away."

"Can you stay long?" Esti asked.

"Not very. If I take the 6:00 o'clock bus to Be'ersheva, I won't be home till 8:30 or so. Your father will have to eat supper alone, and he doesn't like that."

"But you'll stay long enough to see Dov?"

"That's why I came," said her mother brightly.

They sat in the warm kitchen next to golden tea in glasses. Two sad little cakes with bits of crumb and a smear of dried chocolate lay on the plate between them. Esti turned on the oven light and looked at the chicken roasting on a bed of onions, eggplant, and cabbage seasoned with tarragon.

"He'll be home in a little while. He comes home about 3:30 today. He meets with the social worker after school."

"Oh?"

"He's the star of the school, you know. He has this huge bandage on his thigh. And everyone wants to touch it. And they all want to know what it felt like. And ...."

She turned her back upon her mother for a moment. Then she reached for the potholders, opened the squeaky oven door, and took out the pan. Esti wiggled a chicken leg.

"This will be delicious," she said.

"I'm sure it will, but I really can't stay."

"Oh, don't worry," said Esti, "we'll be able to finish this by ourselves, what with lunch and snacks and all."

She put it back in the oven. She sat down. She folded her fingers around the glass of tea to warm them.

"Mom?"

"Yes?"

"I need some help."

"Maybe," said her mother after a moment, "I can take the two of you out to dinner at a little cafe near the central bus station. We can get a bite to eat before I catch my bus. Would you like that?"

Esti smiled. "Dov would like it more than I would. Why don't you take him. Grandmother and grandson together. You can put him on the number 4 bus when you're ready to leave."

"Yes, well ...." But she didn't continue.

"That would give me a chance to study for an exam I have on

Sunday."

"Oh, an exam."

When Esti didn't say anything, her mother continued. "Your father and I didn't want you to stay in Tel Aviv after Gavriel died. You know that. We wanted you to come home, to help in the shop, but no, you knew better. You wanted your own life. Well, people are responsible for the choices they make, Esti. You choose to live here on your own, then you must live here on your own. My place is with your father in Be'ersheva. You can always come back to Be'ersheva and work in the shop."

"I can't go back to Be'ersheva. And you know why."

"We've been through this a hundred times," said Esti's mother solemnly. "I won't have you talk against him."

Esti was quiet.

"That's it, then," she said. "That's all you can do to help me? Invite me to come back to Be'ersheva."

"I don't know what else you want me to do. What else can I do?"

"Think, mother. Imagine."

She watched her mother serenely think. She watched her mother calmly imagine.

"I think that's what I needed to know," Esti said at last.

"What?" asked her mother, afraid that she had given something away for free.

5.

--in a random environment

She opened her eyes. Bars of fluorescent lights, linked together high on the wall, encircled the room and made the greenish walls more ghastly. Her mouth was dry. Her tongue lay thick and adhesive in her mouth.

Arik--was that Arik?--somehow was on the periphery of her vision, but the ghoulish green light hurt her eyes and she was thirsty.

"I'll get that for you," he said. He poured the water into a glass and held the straw to her lips.

"Thanks," she said.

He stood in graceless attendance while she drank from his hand.

"I didn't want to wake you."

"Was I asleep?"

"You look terrible."

"Thanks," she said and closed her eyes.

"So how did it happen?"

"What?" she said.

He wasn't there when she opened her eyes again. She thought perhaps the whole experience had been imagined until she saw the predictably conventional bunch of flowers stuck in a glass without water on her bedside table.

Later in the afternoon, Mira came tentatively through the door. She looked at the people in the five other beds before she recognized Esti by the window.

"So what happened, exactly?" she asked at last.

"I was going to take a test at the university. I got out of the bus and came around to cross at the crosswalk. And this car comes up to pass the bus and just as it gets to the crosswalk the bus backs up--or slides down the hill, I don't know--and bumps me. Of all the people standing there, I'm the one who gets bumped. And suddenly I'm hitting the car and hitting the bus and hitting the road and I wake up here covered with bruises and pain."

"It must really hurt"

"Well," said Esti, "it's only physical."

Eventually Mira said what she had come to say.

"Look, Esti, I really must be going. I've got a sitter for the kids

and I've got to stop at the super before I get home. But I just had to
see how you're doing. And ... and to tell you that there's no need
to hurry back to work because... because Mugrabi has found
someone else to do that 4-11 shift. Bye, now, I really must run.
Feel better. Stop by and see me sometime. I'll give you a free
falafel."

Dinner was served at 5:30 in the open space half-way down the
corridor. Because the space was larger, more open, the light was
less garish. Gray and white television blared in the corner against
the window. The corridor was alive with colored bathrobes and disheveled, slow-moving patients in wrinkled bedclothes. Everyone
who could walk gathered there on crutches and aluminum walkers.
Esti was wheeled out in a chair. She welcomed the protection the
chair gave her against the caroming children brought into the
hospital to visit the sick.

Esti was wheeled up to a table where other patients were eating
or being fed by nurses, volunteers, relatives. A brown plastic tray
was set before her with the promise that someone would be with
her in a minute. She watched the food slowly cool. No one came.
Finally, a sad, young man sat down beside her.

"Is there anything I can do to help you," he said solemnly.

He was so unlike the typical overly cheerful volunteer that she
said, "You can cut my food and help me eat."

And so he did while the details of his body spoke to her. His
eyes fell with intense concentration on the delicacy of cutting her
meat against the grain, on not over-loading her fork with
vegetables, on not spilling her soup. His sober face turned like a
strobe upon her mouth as he lifted the food to her. And when her
own awkwardness of tooth or swollen lip sloshed soup down her
chin, he blotted it so gently with her napkin that she barely felt the
touch. His hazel eyes were alive with amber and golden flecks.

"My name is Shai," he said.

"I'm Esti."

"I'm not ...."

"No. Fine. My fault. I'm not used to eating with a swollen lip. Or being fed."

"What do you do," he asked, "when you're not in the hospital?"

"I'm a graduate student in computer science at the university. And what do you do when you're not feeding invalids in the hospital?"

"I've got a little company that works on sub-contracts from the IAI. We improve the avionics of the F-16, mostly imaging software, and then build mock-ups of the improved versions to train pilots and crew."

"Then you must be up on morphogenesis and the neurophysiological aspects of automata theory."

"That's what I do."

"And you still find time to volunteer in the hospital."

He blushed.

"That's admirable," she said.

He turned his wonderful eyes upon her.

"I was driving the car that hit you," he said. She saw his eyes begin to brim, the amber circle awash in tears which he caught and wiped away with a knuckle.

He helped her back into her bed when the pain of holding herself erect in the chair became unbearable. And he sat with her in the evening, in that ugly garish light, while the families of those who shared the room rattled and chattered around them.

"Suddenly your face was in the window inches from my face and then your body seemed to fill the windshield and then you were gone, flying up against the bus and then falling--it seemed--under my wheels. I never imagined you could survive. I wrenched the wheel to the left, went over a traffic island, and smashed into I-don't-know-what."

"You weren't hurt?"

"No. The car was wrecked."

"What was it?"

"It used to be a Fiat."

Her lip hurt when she smiled.

"I wasn't only surprised," he said, "by the suddenness of your appearance--suddenly you were right there, right before me--but ... by ... the beauty of your face and I remember thinking what's the probability of a face as beautiful as that suddenly appearing in my window, and then, equally suddenly disappearing? And this was mixed up with my realization that I was somehow responsible for its coming and for its going. And I was terrified that I had destroyed that ... your ... beautiful face."

"Beautiful." She had difficulty pronouncing the word.

"Well, okay. Not now. You look like you've been in a prize fight. But this is not the image I see whenever I close my eyes and you appear in my windshield. The image I see is the face that was. And will be again."

She didn't remember all of that evening because her medication had begun to work. But she remembered enough random words and flecks of amber and gold that when she awoke in the morning she could have smiled. And she did.

6.

--probabilistic questions

There are some unexpected days in Tel Aviv, especially in January, when winter forgets it has yet to arrive and summer forgets it has gone. The improbable sky is high and blue, the air crisp, the sun bone-warming and clean, the city washed by the first rains and not yet doused by the dark days of February. War, when there is war, is in another country. Terrorism, when there is terrorism, is far away. Such days tease the spirit with memories of autumn past and expectations of spring to come. Such days are precious, full of celebration. Cats sleep in patches of sunshine. Old ladies, who survived, wearing coats with fur collars bought in Bratislava fifty years before, sit among the brightly forced flowers outside Mon Jardin on Ben Yehuda Street over coffee and cake.

Turned toward the sun, Esti sat among them, her coffee before her. Her plate, with the remnants of chocolate cake, bore the print of the waiter's thumb. Her cane, hanging from the table, did not quite touch the ground. Soon she would abandon that, too, and return to normal life. She smiled to herself. She was sitting in a garden on Ben Yehuda on a sunny morning among the old ladies abloom in winter. What was normal life?

A husband she buried a generation ago and remembers imperfectly from photographs. Frozen forever smiling, drinking tea at a table with friends in army uniform. What would he look like now? Not beneath the ground--quite unrecognizable--but here, walking down a street in Tel Aviv, would she recognize him if he passed her now singing in the sunshine?

And their son, aging unevenly, part baby, part boy, rushing toward adolescence without a male model and with self-destructive violence. He was changing from day to day at various speeds in random directions. Esti watched him, though she didn't understand him. She was cut off from him by his maleness as she was cut off from her mother by her father. She felt herself a generation between, unattached to either the past or the future. Ungenerated by her mother. Ungenerating her son.

She had dealt with--not mastered, no, she wouldn't say mastered--the complications of her ten-years' winter by running on automatic, a Turing machine with a residual soul, connected by maternal love to her son and by filial obligation to her mother. But frozen photographs taught her the limitations of love just as Mira and Mugrabi taught her the limitations of duty.

Esti slipped her fork under the last bite of chocolate cake and confidently lifted it to her mouth.

She was comfortable with the past because she had survived it. The complications of the future concerned her now. Although the accident had revealed no serious problems of morphogenesis, Esti recognized that her feelings for Shai were interconnected with past and future history, her memories and her own projections of what her life was to be.

Esti pressed the back of her fork against the crumbs, leaving the plate free of everything except the chocolate thumbprint.

Shai's feelings were less complicated than hers and more developed. He knew who he was and what he wanted. He said he wanted her. She realized that his exaggerated appreciation of her physical beauty was immersed in guilt. She saw his character marked by effervescent generosity. That was why he showed her around the high-tech facility near Rehovot and introduced her to his family. What were the changing neuro-physiological aspects of her relationship with Shai, wounded as she was by joy now and by torment?

She posed the question as a proposition in automata theory. What was the probability of interconnection for a new woman, freely generated, an elementary automaton unpitted and clean, who was now self-motivated and--(she smiled as her cane fell from the table)--self-propelled?

She lifted her cup and finished the coffee, cold and grainy at the end. Still rich it was with cream, and tasty.

She was accustomed to surviving the winter. Would she be able to survive the spring?

So complicated, this love thing.

Other People's Children

That important morning would have been perfect were it not for other people's children.

He packed the bag and she made the bed. Whenever they stayed here on their way to visit her son, she made the bed before checking out. She knew the chambermaid would silently thank her for leaving the room as tidy as she found it.

She wiped the bathroom sink with a towel and left it neatly folded on the rack. He carried their overnight bag to the door. She carried the tray of rooting seeds and cuttings taken from the garden beneath the boy's window. She refused to leave them in the trunk overnight. The morning heat would wilt them.

As they walked down the hall, the doors opened silently upon an empty elevator, and they stepped right in.

That's the sort of thing she meant by "perfect."

He put their small suitcase into the car. She put the plants, some grown specially for the occasion, in beside her gardening gloves and trowel. The boy would like the flowers when they bloomed. They were his favorites. She always brought them to him.

Although the breakfast room was crowded, they found a small clean table in the No Smoking area. Everyone should control their most annoying habits, she taught, and especially in the morning. How one behaved at breakfast affected other people all day long. But one must be on best behavior at all times.

She took her purse with her to the breakfast table. She disapproved of all that food. Eighteen times during the past eighteen years they had come to visit her son on his special day. They always stayed in the same hotel. She had spoken to the manager more than once about the waste.

For herself she took one roll, one pat of butter, one container of jam--more than enough for anyone's breakfast. She turned a flinty eye on those who piled their plates with food they could not possibly finish.

She was annoyed to discover that, in her absence, a couple had occupied the table next to hers. They had four daughters. Ten, eight, six, and then a two-year-old. Of course. Trying for a son. Even so, she disapproved of excess.

And these were untaught children. The baby, especially. She played with the food that slopped off the side of her plate. She mixed it about with her hands. She put it in her hair.

The parents had brought the children mounds of food, all of the wrong sort.

"Stop that, Nina," said the mother to the six-year-old, "or you can just forget about going to the pool today."

The child wiped her hands on her bathing suit.

"You can spend the rest of the vacation in the room and not have any fun at all."

An empty threat. Quite unsatisfactory.

"Good," said the six-year-old. "I'll watch cable."

"And no television. Now eat nicely, or you won't get any lunch," said the mother, cutting rolls. In some she spread butter and jelly; into others she set sardines, tuna, herring, cheese. She wrapped them in paper napkins and put them in her purse.

No, not very intelligent people. Not at all consistent. That was not the way she had raised her son. Not everyone should be allowed to be a mother.

The father lifted the baby out of the high chair and carelessly wiped her face and hands. The baby walked out between the tables and into the aisle.

"Hello, little girl," said an unpleasant-looking woman who was wearing a loose brown dress over her blue bathing suit and balancing a large plate, much too full of food. "And where are you going?"

"Out to play in the traffic," said the father.

"I thought she was lost," said the lady in the aisle.

"I wish she were," said the father.

"She's so cute."

"You're joking," said the father. "Have you seen her eat?"

"Ha-ha," said the lady. "Do you want to come with me, darling?"

And then the woman actually put her finger into the child's sticky fist.

What a bad example for the other children. Allowing them to go with strangers. Teaching them that their parents don't love them. Children don't understand these foolish adult games.

No, this was no way to raise a child. She had never allowed it in the raising of her own son and she certainly didn't approve when other people did it.

And look at the results. Her son had always been a most perfect child, first in his class in school, first in his company in the army, giving complete satisfaction in every way. Except, of course, for that black morning when he ....

Third Time, Ice Cream

*When you meet a friend unexpectedly three times in one
day, the third time sit and have ice cream together.*

--Israeli custom

The square in Zugarramurdi is a triangle where three roads
meet. One comes up from Dancharinea on the French border, four
kilometers away. One leads off in the direction of Urda, about six
kilometers across the fields, but never arrives there. The third leads
down to the famous cave of witches in Zugarramurdi. Sometimes
tourist buses stop in front of the church to release their passengers
for the walk down to the caves. The buses turn awkwardly in the
triangular square. From the shade of the sycamore trees that cool
the raised patio in front of the Cafe Bar, the stretching, the blinking
of tourists in the heat of the Spanish sun, in the dust and smoke of
the Spanish harvest, take on aspects of the comic and the
grotesque--tortured souls writhing in the smoky fires of hell.

"There's the old woman again," said Adam.

Galit raised her glass of cold Campanas *rosado* and smiled, but
the short figure in black continued across the sunbright square. If
the old woman noticed, she paid no attention. As they descended
the hundreds of stairs to the witches' cave that morning, they met
her briskly coming up and, nodding politely, they greeted her with
"Buenas dias, señora," though she was barely as tall as a
twelve-year-old.

The cave was disappointing: a short open cavern, bright at both ends, with a stream on one side and a great bed of warm gray ash on the other, the remnants of the previous evening's goat-roast for tourists. Later, when they climbed the stairs from the witches' grotto to the farm road above, they decided as they paused for the second time, winded and blown, that the old woman must live there--part goat, part ghost--the scion of a community of women burned as witches in the seventeenth century.

"I really don't believe that story," said Galit.

"Why not?" he said. "Wherever women gathered, from the Middle Ages to the beginning of this century, they were denounced as witches and burned. We've run across it again and again in Europe. And it's not just limited to Christianity. We found the same phenomenon in India and Chile and Mexico and Mozambique before the Christians ever got there."

"Oh," said Galit, "I don't doubt they were denounced and burned."

"There's plenty of evidence," Adam persisted. "Goya drew pictures of them preaching with ears of ass and horns of goat."

"Goya was describing the animal instincts in human nature," said Galit, "and anyway, he was two hundred years after they burned the witches here."

"Okay," conceded Adam, "but the contemporary ecclesiastical records note that many women, old and young, admitted to being witches, to preaching black mass, to being in love with the devil."

"The ecclesiastical records would say that, wouldn't they?"

"Okay, then, what part of the story don't you believe?"

"Well, I don't think religion was the cause; I think it merely justified the murder of women."

"What?"

"Look," said Galit, "not all of these women were old. They didn't all look like witches. Some were young women."

"Witches-in-training?"

"Don't be flippant," she said. "Look, there was a community

of women living in this cave. Yes! Women who ran away from impoverished lives, from slave jobs and cruel husbands; brave women who escaped from the shackles their society imposed on them."

"Here we go," sighed Adam.

"And I think what made these women special is that they were making it. They were herding goats and curing cheese and weaving and carpentering and tinning and doing everything that women did in those days, but they were doing it for themselves! That's why they were killed, don't you see? Not because they worshipped the devil, but because they were a community living successfully outside the conventions society defined for women. And that's why the church had to brand them as witches, so that it could burn them as a lesson and a warning to all other women who might want the same thing. These women were killed not because they were witches, but because they were free."

"Very interesting. You're such a rationalist, Galit. More wine?"

"Are you trying to irrationalize me?"

Adam laughed as he tipped the cold *rosado* into her glass.

"How did she manage to escape, then?" he said, indicating the old woman in black who had once again entered the triangular square.

"Ask her."

"'Third time, ice cream,'" said Adam, rising to address the old woman.

"Adam, don't."

But he was already into the smoky sunshine. She saw him approach the old woman who stopped and looked at him and looked over at Galit in the shade and, inclining her head slightly, returned to the patio with him. As the old woman gathered her skirts to sit at their table, Galit noticed her hair was as black as her clothes and her skin was as white as cave-grown mushrooms.

The waiter greeted her as Doña Estella and brought another glass for her and another bottle.

"Where are your children?" asked Doña Estella with old, clear eyes and a level view.

"We have no children," said Galit.

"We work for an airline," Adam added, "and spend much of our time traveling. It's no life for a child."

"Do you have children," Galit asked.

"I have six," Estella said.

"How nice for you."

"I don't know where four of them are buried. They died in the troubles of 1938. One was buried there," she indicated the churchyard behind her, "before she was baptized. My husband lies there, too."

"And where is the sixth child," Adam asked since Galit was too pale to do so.

"He lives in the north."

"Does he visit you often?"

"He cannot return."

"Can't you visit him?"

"I have never been to the north."

"It's a beautiful country," said Galit recovering, "you really must go there sometime. France is almost as beautiful as Spain."

"And Paris is almost as beautiful as Madrid," Adam added.

"I have never been to Madrid," said Estella.

"Well, then," said Adam, appealing to the prejudice of the provincial, "it's almost as beautiful as Pamplona, the capital of Navarra!"

But when her face remained unmoved, he added, "The fiesta of San Fermin?"

"The church is rich," she said, "in saints."

"You've never been to Pamplona?" Adam was gentle.

"I have been to Dancharinea," she said, "a large town. And I have walked to Urda across the fields to see the sister of my husband while she was still alive. And once," she said, "when I was much younger, before the troubles, we went by cart to Elizonda."

Adam poured her another glass of wine. She drank and smacked her lips appreciatively.

"And where do you live?" she said warmly. "Your Spanish is not from the valley of Baztan."

"We fly out of Tel Aviv," Adam said.

Estella looked at him as if the words had no sound.

"We come from Israel," Galit added.

Estella sat perfectly still, her little girl's face immobile as she stared at them, waiting for an answer.

"Actually," Galit continued, "we live in Jerusalem."

Suddenly alight, Estella clasped her hands above her breast and turned her shining face to the sky.

"Jerusalem," she said, reverently.

"Yes, we ...." But Galit touched his arm.

"Jerusalem," Estella continued in adoration. Her gaze descended from the blank white sky to the faces of the children before her. Slowly, as if afraid to dissipate the vision, she unclasped her hands, and slowly her black sleeve stretched, slowly her white hand reached out to touch the substance of one who came from Jerusalem.

"From Jerusalem," she whispered.

"Yes," said Adam, "we live in Jerusalem."

"Tell me about Jerusalem," Estella said. "I have only seen it in my mind."

"It's a very hilly city," said Adam, "like the mountain towns of Navarre, only larger, of course."

"What is it like to walk on streets paved with gold?"

Galit was first to answer.

"Well," she said, "the buildings are made of Jerusalem stone which seems to glow like pink gold in the late afternoon light."

"And are the mansions of the Lord large and stately?"

"Some are," said Adam with a giggle, "but we live in a small apartment."

"And when you leave Jerusalem, you fly, you actually fly?"

"Yes," said Adam seriously, "El Al, out of Tel Aviv."

"If ever I come to live in Jerusalem," Estella said, "I would never leave. I would only fly in Jerusalem. But tell me," she said, "what are the other people like in Jerusalem?"

"Well, they're mostly Jews," said Galit.

"Jews?"

"Yes, Jerusalem is the capital of Israel, the Jewish state."

But the old woman was remembering.

"Once we had Jews in Zugarramurdi," she said, "but the black priest came and sat in the black chair beside the altar. It is there. You can see it. He brought all the Jews of Zugarramurdi before him. They were a dirty people. They stole, they cheated, they drank blood of goats and children. And once they admitted all their crimes, he burned them in the square."

They looked across the angular square and up to the church on the other side where the inquisitor sat in his black chair beside the black altar. The smoke of innocent harvest fires was in the air.

"*We* are Jews," said Galit.

The old woman turned toward Galit and regarded her with eyes the color of a smoky sky.

"Oh," she said, "then you know how wicked the Jews are."

Burn

Some say the world will end in fire,
Some say in ice.

The three young men came easily up the four flights of stairs to the top floor of the decrepit apartment house in Alexandria. They wore ragged coats, the wretched refuse of Goodwill Industries. The oldest wore a frizzled plaid hunter's jacket with pockets long since distended by shotgun shells. The tallest wore a navy-blue pea-coat with two buttons missing. And the hardiest wore only the furry acrylic lining of a khaki winter coat.

They were unaccustomed to wearing coats at all, inured to heat or cold by burning desert suns and freezing desert nights, but they wore coats in the Washington area in order to look like everyone else and so disappear among the tourists and the street people in the DC subway or the crowds of students that hungered around Howard or Georgetown University.

They found the door they wanted. One of them raised a red hand burned raw by the winter wind and knocked firmly. They could hear laughter and the woman's voice raised. It was she who opened the door, her face bright with smiles. Her smile froze in the cold air that swept in from the hall, her face sobered, her eyes looked demurely at their shoes, she backed submissively away into the room behind the door.

"Good afternoon, Basma. We have come to speak to Amir."

"Salam," she said, holding the door open for them.

They walked past her into the living room. A thin, bookish boy was sitting on the sofa, sewing a button onto the shirt across his knees. Amir bundled the shirt into the open sewing basket at his feet.

"Salam Alaikim," he said, rising to greet them.

"Salam," said Tariq.

"Salam," said Abdallah and Salim.

A few books bound in golden leather, their titles burned in black on the red Morocco spines, lay athwart the coffee table. Amir quickly stacked and handed them, together with the basket, to Basma. Then the four young men made themselves comfortable on the shabby, graduate-student sofa and chairs.

"I see you have been in America too long," said Tariq.

"No. Only four years," said Amir. "But my thesis is finished now and we are going home in three months."

"About libraries, right?" asked Salim.

"Yes," said Amir. "Western Influence upon the Philosophy and Design of Library Collections in the Third World."

"Very interesting."

"Yes," Amir smiled. "I show that the design of western library collections is antithetical to the needs and purposes of the libraries in emerging nations. They emphasize technology and privilege Western values at the expense of the local cultures and the values that built those cultures." Amir sat back comfortably and smiled.

"That's not what I meant at all," said Tariq.

Amir's smile faded. He looked at Tariq, suddenly aware of a threat sitting with iron verticality before him. Tariq was physically larger than Amir and older, more politically alert. His physical appearance was a disparaging reminder of their purpose for being in the United States. Since he held his head high and viewed the world from either side of a great thin hooked nose, his mien was arrogant, his bearing contemptuous. His demeanor affirmed the dignity of their shared ancient cultures in the context of fast food and plastic. Tariq's eye measured them constantly and always with the distaste of an artisan obliged to work against his will with slightly defective materials.

Amir looked at him with the tightening apprehension of those who know they are tested and being failed for reasons they can not understand.

"You have been too long in the west," Tariq continued. "You insult Islamic womanhood."

Amir was confounded. What was the connection between the philosophy of libraries and Islamic womanhood?

"Don't you realize," Tariq said, "that when you lower yourself to do the work of women, you not only abrogate your own dignity, but you rob women of their nobility? When you take from them the occupation that defines their dignity, you might as well cut their hair and sell them as whores and slaves."

"But my thesis has nothing to do with the nobility of women."

"I wasn't talking about your thesis."

Amir was lost.

"I was talking," said Tariq with crushing finality, "about your sewing on a button."

Basma entered the silent room with four small porcelain cups and tiny saucers on a round brass tray with an elegantly carved Turkish coffee pot of engraved brass. She set the tray in the center of the coffee table--four wooden crates covered with a square of lacquered plywood under a red-and-white checkered cloth. She returned to the silent room with a plate of rich pastry melting in a golden sugary syrup. She sat beside her husband on the sofa and poured the hot Turkish coffee into the tiny porcelain cups and handed them around, acknowledging their thanks with a shy smile. She smiled even more shyly as they honored her with extravagant compliments on the pastry. When all were served, she rose and left the room.

"Thank you, Basma," they said.

"I am glad to see," said Tariq at last, "that you have not taken all of a woman's honor from her."

Amir sipped his sweet coffee with satisfaction.

"But I am surprised," Tariq continued, "to see the Jordanian keffiah, which has so often stanched the blood of our martyred Palestinian brothers, used as a table cloth in your house."

Amir looked with horror at the red-and-white fringed keffiah that covered the coffee table while Tariq stared at him with humorless eyes.

"I will beat my wife for this outrage," said Amir.

"No need. What happens in your house is your responsibility, not your wife's. Basma is only a woman. You are the man. But ...."

"Yes," said Amir eagerly.

"Perhaps, if it is not too much to ask," said Tariq, "I might have an ashtray?"

Amir rose and went to the kitchen door. They heard him say, "Basma, bring an ashtray for Tariq. Hurry."

As he sat down again, Amir explained with a smile, "We don't normally have ashtrays around anymore because none of our American friends smoke."

They looked at him in silence.

"We are not your American friends," said Abdallah at last, but it was Tariq who saved the situation and to whom Amir was grateful.

"Yes. The refusal of the Americans to smoke," Tariq said as he struck a match and torched the cigarette in his mouth, "is a further example of the decadence of their society."

They waited.

"Refusing to smoke is a cowardly act. Americans worship life. It is obvious in their dedication to materialism, to creature comforts and living well. They think living is all there is to life. Since they can't see anything more important than life, they are limited to the safe and the protected. They don't think anything is worth dying for. They are blind to martyrdom. They have no principles--except, perhaps, the principle of personal pleasure. But they can't even give themselves to the pleasures of smoking. How can they possibly give themselves to anything more important? Martyrdom is no longer a possibility for Americans."

"And that's why," said Salim, "we shall win in the end."

"Yes," said Abdallah.

"Yes," said Tariq. "We shall win because we are willing to die.

Americans are not. Americans are afraid of everything--of cholesterol and salt and prepared foods and apples and pollution. They are afraid of being too fat and being too thin. They are afraid of the air they breathe."

"They are soft," said Salim.

"They train their men to love comfort and money," Tariq continued, "and they train their women to be whores. Salim himself has had six American women already, and he has only been in the country for two years."

"Decadent," sniffed Abdallah.

"They dishonor women," said Tariq. "They destroy the family. They are avaricious wasters of the world's natural resources which they transform to trash for their aggressive consumers. They replace love with sex and religion with football."

Tariq lifted his mighty arm. He placed the cigarette between his thin lips. He drew a great breath as the cigarette end grew dangerously bright. The ash fell from the cigarette and tumbled down the front of his plaid coat. He brushed it away with contempt and crushed the cigarette in the ashtray, twisting it, grinding it.

"If only we could do something," prompted Abdallah, "like your countryman, Mohammed Salameh."

"To affirm the sanctity of Islam against the decadence of American values," said Salim.

"And strike a blow against the American-Zionist presence in Palestine," said Abdallah.

"Especially now," said Salim, "since the American rape of Baghdad and the butchery of our women and children."

"Did you know," Abdallah asked, "that all the American pilots who bombed Iraq were Jews? Did you see them laughing?"

They sat quietly for a moment. Tariq took another cigarette from his pack and lit it.

"We have not been called to martyr ourselves," Tariq said as he concentrated on the cigarette in his hand, turning it this way and that, "but even we can do something to hasten the triumph of Islam and register our disgust at the immorality and decadence of

American society. Salim, for instance, delivers pizzas. Tell Amir what you do, Salim."

"When I deliver pizzas at night, I open the lid of the box and do this." He touched a long finger to the side of his nose and suddenly snorted. A wad of snot shot into the palm of his other hand. He held it up for all to see.

"Let the Americans eat their pizza," he said. "They never know the difference." He wiped his palm against his pant-leg.

The three young men looked at Amir. They were not smiling any more. They seemed huge to him, enormous. They filled the room.

"And what have you done, Amir, to express your contempt for this degenerate American culture?"

Amir faltered, "I ...."

"Have done nothing," finished Abdallah.

"What can I do? I'm a student. I have been working on my thesis. In another few months I return to my country. I am eager to make a statement for the Americans to remember forever, but what can I do?"

"You too have a job." They watched him in silence. They waited.

"Yes," he said.

They looked at him. They waited for him to continue.

"It's part of my work/study program," Amir said.

They waited for him, watching. The smoke curled toward the ceiling in the still air.

"I work in the library."

"And what work do you do in this library?"

"I shelve books. When people are finished, I pick up the books and return them to the shelves. It's a job of great responsibility." And then he admitted softly, "I get to touch all the books and put them in the right place."

"What library is this?"

"The Library of Congress."

"The Library of Congress," said Tariq, drawing deeply on his cigarette. He tapped the end against the ashtray, but the fiery head came off the defective cigarette and burned brightly for a moment. Tariq watched it and expelled his mighty lungs full of smoke toward Amir.

2.

From what I've tasted of desire
I hold with those who favor fire.

When their guests had gone, Basma opened the windows in the living room to let in the wintry air. Then she cleared away the dishes and the mounded ashtray. She carried the dishes into the little kitchen. She carefully folded up the corners of the red-checked cloth on the coffee table and took it out to the back stairs and shook it out over the wooden railing. She hung it to air on the clothesline. She wiped the top of the coffee table with a sponge. She emptied the ashtray into the garbage bag beneath the sink. She carried the half-full garbage bag down the back stairs and put it into the garbage can behind the building. She pressed the lid down firmly.

When she returned to the living room, Amir was closing the windows. The billow fell out of the cheap cotton curtains; they hung limply in the cold room.

"What are you doing, Basma? Have you lost your mind?"

"I wanted to get the smell of the smoke out of the house."

"Must we die of the cold for a little smoke?"

"They are very nice friends, but I wish they wouldn't smoke so much. It smells terrible and stays in the curtains and clothes for days."

"It's freezing."

"Shall I get you a sweater?"

"No." He frumped in a chair.

She went into the kitchen to prepare their dinner. But she came back into the living room with a sweater for him. He had the leather-bound books in his lap.

"What did they want?"

"Who?"

"Tariq and the others."

"It is political," Amir said to the books.

She was silent, waiting.

"But what is it?" she said.

"It is political," he said, looking at her.

She returned to the kitchen.

Later, as they sat over dinner on the pull-down table in the tiny kitchen, she said, "You've hardly said a word all evening."

"I've been thinking."

"About defending your thesis?"

"No."

She was silent, waiting.

"What are you thinking about, then?" she said at last.

"The library." He looked up at her and smiled. "I love the library," he said.

"Yes. I sometimes think it is like a mistress. You love it more than you love me."

"I will miss working there."

"But you will be working at the university library when we get home. You will be building the library, establishing it according to the principles you set out in your thesis."

"Yes," he said, "but the library in Irbid is a poor library. Nothing compares to what the Americans have here. The Library of Congress is rich and beautiful."

"You're working there until the very last moment. You work Tuesday afternoon and we leave early Wednesday morning."

"Still ...," he said.

They were silent for a while as they broke off pieces of pita and dipped them into tehina with olive oil and pignoli nuts sprinkled with paprika.

"The Library of Congress, do you know what that is?"

"It's for all the books in America."

"Yes, of course. But no, it's more than that--not only the repository for books. It preserves the sum-total of American wisdom, culture, civilization. It is the record of everything that was dreamed or thought in America. And as such it is ... it is ... the symbol of America. America itself. It holds the heart and soul of America."

The light that she loved was in his eyes. She admired the passion of his commitment which set him apart from the others and led to his winning the scholarship to study in America. It was the special part, the iron part, of the gentle boy she fell in love with, the source of her security and the flintstone of her happiness.

"And someone who can put a knife in that heart will live forever," said Amir. "He is the one, they will say, he is the one who put a knife in the depraved heart of America and struck a blow for the liberation of Palestine."

"You frighten me when you talk like that," said Basma surprised.

"There is nothing to be afraid of. It's completely safe."

She waited for him to continue, but he didn't. Finally, she asked, "What did they want?"

He turned on her. "I'm a little angry at you," he said.

"Why?"

"For using a keffiah on the coffee table."

She looked down at the half-eaten pita before her and was silent.

"You didn't seem to mind," she said at last, "when I put it there two years ago."

"Well, I mind now."

"What did they want?"

"It is political," he said.

"Oh--be careful of your sweater. You got some tehina on it." She reached over with a napkin to wipe the food from his sleeve. "Here, let me ...."

He stood up, his face red with rage.

"You have lived here too long," he said. "You have become

American. You think only of clothes now. What do I care if there's a spot of food on this damn sweater. It's not important. Don't you understand!"

He roughly pulled the sweater over his head, stretching it cruelly. She bowed her head.

"Here's what I think of your sweater."

He threw the sweater into her field of vision and stomped on it.

"You think because we are in America you can ask anything you want about your husband's business. It is my business. It is not your business. It is important. Not sweaters. It is political, I tell you, political. And when we get home, you will have to change your ways--and remember that I am the man in this house."

He turned out of the kitchen. She heard him take his coat from the closet and close the front door. She slowly reached down to pick up the twisted sweater. She untangled it and folded it carefully. When she hugged it to her burning face, she blotted a tear. The sweater smelled of smoke.

3.

But if it had to perish twice,
I think I know enough of hate
To say that for destruction ice
Is also great

The name beside the bell read Mustapha el-Aqsa Aziz, an Egyptian student of Education who had returned three years earlier. Amir pressed the bell. Salim came to the door and led Amir through a littered hall to the apartment. It was smaller than his own and smelled of *ful* and curry and lacked the amenities of married life. Three mattresses without sheets lay on the floor in the living room, littered with crumpled clothes and twisted blankets. The smell reminded him of the warm odor of goat in the shed behind his grandfather's house. Dirty cups and smeared paper plates littered the surfaces of the orange crates that served for tables. The windows were bare except for the beige roll-down shades, tattered at the edges and stained.

"Salam, Amir," said Tariq.

"Salam Alaikim."

After Abdallah brought in the coffee in a burnished aluminum pot, they sat cross-legged or reclined on the mattresses. The cold winter sun played upon the blinds and suffused the room with the yellow light of a campfire. The smoke from four cigarettes rose toward the ceiling in the still air--white smoke in the yellow light.

"Tell me about the Library of Congress," said Tariq.

"There are three buildings connected by an underground tunnel. The Adams building houses Education. The Jefferson building holds literature, philosophy, history, genealogy, and rare books. It's an old building and being renovated now. And the Madison building has all the periodicals--newspapers and magazines that go back to the 18th century."

"All the way back to the 18th century?" said Salim, amused.

"And you work ...."

"I work in Jefferson, but I have access to the stacks in all the buildings."

"Not everyone can go into the stacks," said Abdallah. "I tried once and was told I'd need a pass."

"I work in the stacks," said Amir.

"What," asked Tariq, "are you allowed to bring into the library?"

"My briefcase. My lunch box. My coat. Anything."

"And what are you allowed to bring into the stacks?"

"The same."

"Don't you have a locker or something?"

"No. The lockers are for the people who use the library on a regular basis. Workers in the library have a room where we leave our coats and belongings while we work. Right behind Circulation."

"They don't check you coming in?"

"No," said Amir, "only on the way out."

"The Americans are so stupid," said Abdallah. "It never occurs to them that someone might try to take something into the library. They only think someone might steal their precious belongings."

"Yes. Their stupidity is their weakness; their naïveté is our strength. Amir!"

"Yes, Tariq."

"I am calling upon you in the name of the Arab Nation and in the holy name of Islam."

"I am ready to die for Islam and the Arab Nation."

"Your martyrdom is not necessary."

"I am willing to die to restore Palestine to glory."

"Your death would accomplish nothing. It is more important that you escape. The Arab Nation needs intellectuals like you."

"Escape?"

4.

And would suffice.
--Robert Frost

"Good morning, Mr. Fitzgerald."

"Good morning, Amir. Last day, eh?"

"Yes, it is."

"Going back home, are you?"

"Yes. Tomorrow morning."

"Where is your home, India?"

"Jordan."

"Well, I hope you've enjoyed yourself here in the U. S. of A. and that you have a safe trip crossing over the river Jordan. Ha-ha. We'll miss you."

"Thank you, Mr. Fitzgerald."

"Have a nice day."

Amir went up the stairs, past the Reading Room, past the card catalogues, past the banks of computer terminals, and through the staff door into the stacks. He climbed up half a floor to the staff room and hung his coat on the hooks along the wall.

"Hi, Amir."

"Hi, Amir, last day?"

"Yes."

"Well, make it a good one," said Jack.

"Okay, guys. Let's do it," said Morty.

They attached their Walkmans to their belts, set the earphones on their heads, adjusted the volume and the bass/treble balance, picked a trolley, and pushed it out into the stacks. Morty and Jack listened to rock-n-roll and traded tapes half-way through the day. Melissa, Liu, and Fred started at 12:00 and listened to classical music. Sometimes, when he turned off his own Walkman of Arabic music in a very quiet area of the stacks, Amir could tell who was working near him by the music he heard.

Before Amir left the room, he took his green Sears thermos from his lunch box and set it on a trolley of books to be shelved in the northeast corner of level A, the top floor of the stacks. Once the fire started it would burn down as well as up. Early in the morning or late in the afternoon were the best times. Fewer busybodies were in the stacks then. Transient busybodies were in the Library of Congress for a day or a week. Permanent busybodies lived in the DC area and had carrels or permanent stack passes. Transients asked the stupider questions.

He took the elevator to A floor and wheeled out into the corridor. At this time of day there would be only one permanent busybody here--a woman of indefinite age who had an open carrel and always arrived dragging a two-wheeled luggage carrier with three matched pieces of yellow luggage. One was a box of file-folders elaborately tabbed. One was an IBM portable computer with dot-matrix printer attachment which she plugged into the wall and turned on. The third was a carry-on bag that seemed to contain all her personal belongings from which she took note pads, pencils, erasers, tipp-ex, and a ruler. She spread all this material around her among her open books, each in their accustomed place, together with the day's file folder of work. Then she folded her arms on the desk, lay her head down, and slept for eight hours. No one had ever seen her do anything other than sleep. At the end of the day, she packed up her folders and paraphernalia, unplugged her computer, loaded up her two-wheeled baggage carrier, and disappeared.

Although she was safe, Amir avoided her.

The main corridors were brightly lit; the side aisles which held the stacks of books were dark. Amir wheeled his trolley into an aisle, flipping the switch in the corridor that lit the aisle. The lights were on a timer; after five minutes, they would automatically turn off. He started to shelve the books. He worked for four minutes. He stopped. He listened intently. He heard nothing. He unscrewed the cup of his thermos. The silvered glass bottle it should have contained had been removed. He pulled out cotton batting until he found the small incendiary device, no larger than a pack of cigarettes. The light in the aisle switched off. He turned a switch to "I" which activated the pre-set timer. He pressed a button. A tiny red light glowed. The bomb was armed and set. Using the trolley to shield him from the corridor, he bent and placed the bomb in the hollow space between the rows of books on the bottom shelf of the stack. He stuffed the batting back in the thermos, screwed on the top, and set it on the trolley. He went to the corridor and turned on the light in the aisle.

He ran his fingers lovingly over the stippled texture of the book he took from the cart. The book beside it had marbled end-papers slightly marred by foxing. The ancient maroon leather of the next book was worn along the spine but the gold-leaf edging was intact. He looked at all the books on the trolley, length, breadth, thickness, and color. And then he heard the thrilling music and tingling words of the *nasheed* in the earphones. He continued shelving the books.

At lunch time he put the thermos back in his lunch box and left the Jefferson building by the back door, the only doors that were open during the renovations. He crossed the parking lot, waited for a break in the dangerous traffic on 2nd Street, and crossed to the

Adams building.

On the Independence Street side of Adams was a grassy knoll where the street people collected in the sun--the wracked refuse of America's teeming shores. They were mostly immobile, sitting lump-like in their layered coats or lying on newspapers in the thin sun. They were alone and wrapped in misery, the inevitable conclusion of American individualism, the ultimate in self-reliance. They defended with passive authority the shopping bags containing their belongings which they distributed on the ground close around them. Anyone, of course, could steal anything from any of them since they were among the most powerless of the mighty Americans. But they had nothing worth stealing. Some had two-wheeled grocery carts made of wire; others had discarded baby-carriages; the wealthiest had stolen shopping carts, dangling plastic sacks and heaped with the detritus of American culture. This was the predictable end of American acquisitiveness. The clothes, the fashions, the food, the people--all disposable. How different from the support of the extended family and veneration of the elderly he was accustomed to.

Tariq was sitting at one of the tables between the Adams building and the grassy area littered with street people. He had already laid out his sandwiches and a green Sears thermos.

"Salam," they said to each other.

"How did it go?"

"Well," said Amir.

"Good."

Amir opened his lunch box and unwrapped a pita stuffed with humus, salad, pickle. He set his thermos on the table. They ate quietly, Tariq pouring hot tea into both of their cups from a red Wagner thermos. At the end of the meal, Amir put Tariq's green Sears thermos into his own lunch box while Tariq packed away Amir's thermos. They threw their crusts and paper refuse into a huge wire rubbish container beneath a sign that said "Throw your garbage here."

The street people began to move, a slow and sluggish

movement of shopping bags and shopping carts in the direction of the garbage bins. It was lunch time for everyone.

Late in the afternoon, Amir took a trolley of books to be shelved on level 32. As he wheeled the trolley over to the south-west corner, he was surprised to hear Stravinsky's "The Rite of Spring" in the south-central section. Melissa. He slipped past the aisle in which she was working and found the aisle he was looking for. He turned on the light and started to shelve the books. The light went off after five minutes. He came out to the corridor to turn it on again. Four minutes later, with the trolley between him and the corridor, he opened the thermos and took out the cotton batting. He slipped the incendiary device out of the empty thermos. He turned the timing switch to "I." The light in the aisle went off. He pressed the button which armed the device and placed the bomb in the hollow space between the books on the bottom row as Melissa appeared in the bright light of the corridor.

"Here he is," she said, turning on the light in the aisle.

"Okay, Amir," said Jack as he swung past Melissa from the corridor into the aisle. "This is your last trolley, my boy. You're wanted in the staff room. Now."

"It's not 4:30 yet."

"I don't care. Some people are waiting for you and they're pretty impatient."

"Let me just finish ...."

"Now means now--not later. Just leave your trolley under the window over there and come on."

"I'd really ...."

"No arguments--Oh, I see. Trying to hide the evidence."

"No."

"I'm a witness," said Jack. "Drinking tea in the stacks is a federal offense. They'll put you in jail and throw away the key. You'd better bring that." He pointed at Amir's thermos standing in two parts on the trolley. "You're not coming back."

Amir quickly screwed the top back on.

"Let's go. You're under arrest."

Jack pulled Amir's trolley roughly out of the aisle and set it against the window in the corridor.

"Did you really think you could get away with it?" he said.

He shepherded Amir along the corridor to the elevator. He pressed the button for the elevator. The call button glowed red. When the elevator door opened, Morty was inside.

"I've got him," said Jack.

"Good thing, too," said Morty, who pressed the button for the 28th level where the staff room was.

When the door opened on the 28th level, Liu was there.

"We've got him."

"I wondered where you were. They're waiting for him."

There was no place to run. Amir accepted his martyrdom with quiet dignity and resignation to the will of Allah.

Jack held him by one arm, Morty by the other, as he entered the staff room. He saw Mr. Fitzgerald from Security and two of the other security officers. People from personnel and circulation and the research desk were all standing around looking at him, staring at him.

They opened their mouths and everyone started to shout at him at the same time. Only when he saw the work-table spread with food, did he realize they were singing "For He's A Jolly Good Fellow."

The Lame Woman's Child

The three young men spoke in low voices beneath the tree on the shady side of the apartment house. The two in shorts and sandals leaned upon their elbows in the grass. The fair-skinned boy with a crooked smile and red hair aglow in the half light sat upright, his back against the tree, his red beret tucked in his epaulette, his combat boots crossed in front of him. Though they sat in a circle, they seemed to face him. The girl in brown uniform with a green leaf on her shoulder patch sat cross-legged among them. Her head was down and her heavy black hair fell before her face. She picked fallen twigs out of the grass. She slit the bark with a thumbnail. She peeled the bark away.

"I don't actually *know*," said Uzi, "but I can guess."

"How come you suddenly got so smart?" Danny asked, his mouth awry in amusement.

"Well, first you're quiet for a day or two and then you disappear. Then there's a commando raid in Tunis. They kill Abu Jihad. Worldwide television, radio, newspapers. Then you come back and you don't know anything. You've been somewhere in the desert on maneuvers, you say. You haven't heard a thing."

"What does that prove?" asked Tamar from beneath her helmet of hair. She was always the most skeptical.

"Then there was that raid into Lebanon," Uzi continued. "Again, you're quiet, then you disappear. They bring back that Hizbullah sheik, Abdul Karim Oved. And then you come back and we have to tell you all about it. You never heard anything. You're the most uninformed or the most ignorant officer in the entire army."

"I'm always quiet," Danny whispered.

"No, he means seriously quiet," Shimon whispered.

"I'm always seriously quiet," Danny whispered. "That's why women love me."

"Name one!" Shimon challenged. "Other than Tamar."

"Tamar's not a woman," Uzi added, "she's a captain."

Tamar looked up from eviscerating the twig. Her straight black hair fell across half her face.

"Then a group of our boys takes a walk in the Bakaa to look for Ron Arad," Shimon said. "One person hurt lightly. And where's Danny? Recuperating at Tel HaShomer."

"A training accident."

"Yes, of course," Shimon was ironic. "You tore up your leg in a jump. Right."

They sat quietly for a moment. Tamar peeled back the thin bark from another twig lying in the grass. The smooth white wood glowed.

"You're the only soldier in the history of the Israeli army who doesn't have any stories to tell," Uzi challenged. "Nothing every happens to you."

"My mother said," Shimon started, and they all looked at him. "My mother said that the country owes you a debt of gratitude it can never repay."

"I'm in love with your mother," Danny laughed.

"Everyone's in love with Shimon's mother," Uzi leered.

Shimon rapped his knuckles on Uzi's head.

"Hello? Anybody home?" he said.

"Come on," said Danny "It's me you're talking about, not Rambo or double-oh-seven."

"Double-oh-Danny."

"Well," said Shimon, "if you won't admit it, there's one person here who can settle the argument."

They looked at Tamar.

"Don't tell me, Tamar," Shimon continued, "that you never

pulled his file up on the screen."

"You don't tell me what you pull," she parried, "and I won't tell you what I pull."

"Ohhhh-ohhhh," groaned Uzi, rolling off his elbow and onto his back. "Help me, God!"

"Come on, Tamar, we're not asking for the secret of the holy of holies at Gelilot. Just ... you know ... the truth about Danny."

"Be a sweetheart, Tamar," said Uzi.

"Don't be a bitch," said Shimon.

The window of the apartment above their heads opened and a mother's voice called out, "Danny!"

Danny stood briskly and came out from under the shadow of the tree into the shadow of the building.

"Your father is awake. He wants to see you. Come."

"I'm going up, too," said Tamar rising.

"Oh sweet Tamar, don't leave us!" cried Shimon.

"Oh lovely Tamar," cried Uzi, "is Danny really a hero or am I just a shit-head?"

Tamar turned around a pillar to the building and flashed the smile they occasionally dreamt of.

"Yes," she said. And disappeared into the building.

2.

As Tamar followed Danny up the stairs, she asked, "How is he?"

"No change," he said. "There can never be any change. It's inevitable."

When they got to the third landing, Danny turned to face her before she went into her apartment.

"It didn't occur to me ...," he started. And then he said, "How much do you know, Tami?"

As she turned to answer, the light in the hall went off. They stood in darkness. In silence.

Finally, Danny said, "Tamar?"

"I know what you've told me," she said.

"You never pulled my file?"

When she didn't answer, he pressed the timer that lit the hall. Suddenly she was there before him, looking directly at him, her thick hair flung straight back from her eyes.

"Tamar, I don't have to tell you. You, of all people. It's dangerous to know too much."

"I know what I need to know," she said.

"Tamar."

"What do you think I do?" she said, quickly. "It's my job to know."

"Listen to me. Some things it's better not to know."

"Thank you, daddy," she said.

He threw a fake punch at her face, but instead of ducking, she blocked his fist with a crisp forearm parry and moved inside. When his arms didn't fall about her shoulders, she quickly changed to pummeling his stomach a little harder than he expected.

"Ohhh," he moaned comically as he fell back against the elevator door with a crash. "Help me, God!"

The door to Tamar's apartment opened and her mother leaned out. Hedva's golden hair swirled about her face.

"Tami? Is that you?" Hedva asked. "Oh, Danny. How's Ayelet today?"

"Fine," said Danny.

"Ask her to come to me later for coffee," Hedva said. "You're invited too. I have a nice poppyseed cake. Tell her."

Danny and Tamar turned toward their parents' apartments as the light in the hall went out.

The room in which Danny's father was dying was always brightly lit. All day the lights burned as Nimrod dozed toward death. All night the window blazed in the building, a beacon for travelers and flying insects. Nimrod Benzion ordered the pictures removed from the walls to increase the light. That was how Danny discovered where the concrete block had been hollowed out and a *Rav-Bariach* safe set into the wall.

Danny's mother, with sleeves rolled and silver hair tied in a kerchief, came out of the room carrying smeared cotton clouts and washcloth and the basin of warm dirty water. Ayelet walked with the irregular lurch of the maimed, her left leg having been severed below the knee in a traffic accident of her youth in which three of her friends died. Only Hedva and Ernu walked away virtually untouched. And then they married. And then, later than expected, Tamar was born.

Danny stood aside to let his mother pass, as though to honor the excrement of the dying.

"See if you can get him to eat something," Ayelet said. "I've chopped up some dates for him on a plate there."

As Danny came through the door, his father's head rolled on the pillow toward him and smiled. Fortunately, his teeth were in. Danny could barely understand him when he spoke without his teeth. His glasses in a black plastic frame were much too large for his ravaged face. His head was bald from the chemicals and the shiny skin of his scalp was brilliant with reflected light.

Nimrod should have been Danny's grandfather. When he couldn't find his wife and children after the war in Europe, he devoted fifteen years to revenge in Argentina. He believed that any German who escaped to South America was guilty of something. Nimrod's freight business transferred their belongings from storage in Europe to new homes in South America. And then, long after they settled comfortably into new lives, the house caught fire in the middle of the night, or the car exploded--cars exploded those days in South America--or the husband simply disappeared and no one ever found the newly turned earth in the vast savanna.

Only after he helped transport Eichmann to Israel did Nimrod decide to abandon vengeance to the professionals, sell his business, and move to Israel. He married Ayelet, already maimed and almost twenty-five years his junior, and then Danny was born perhaps a bit too quickly.

Danny sat in the only chair in the room and looked at the man old enough to be his grandfather.

"I hate this," Nimrod said in a gravely voice without energy. "I hate having her ... change my diapers and ... wipe my ass."

Nimrod's lungs were high, tight, and fragile, the tiny sacs corrupt with cancer. They could hemorrhage at any moment, and he would drown in his own blood before they could save him.

"I regret nothing," he said. "Nothing."

Not the children caught in the roaring, crackling house? Not the mother dismembered when her husband started the car? Not the veteran with the empty sleeve who wept uncontrollably?

Danny looked at the man who regretted nothing and was silent.

"I hate dying," Nimrod said. "It's boring," he said, "waiting for the body ... to stop."

He looked at Danny.

"It was easier to fight ... to be alive ... when I knew ... who the enemy was.... who was trying to kill me.... Now," he said, "I am my own ... enemy."

The old man took his eyes off his son and stared at the ceiling. Danny knew he would soon lose focus, drift off to doze. Nimrod was practicing for death. His eyes would glaze, his words become less connected. And he would sleep.

"You know every death," Nimrod said. "Soon you will know ... my death, too.... Only," he said, "you don't know ... every life.... All my life."

The old man broke his drift with a smile. He had snagged on a memory. Danny watched him.

"Important to know," he said. "I want you to ... take care," he said, "of Hedva and ...."

Seeing his father slip into confusion and nonsense--he must have meant Ayelet--Danny leaned forward with the plate of cut dates.

"Have something to eat, father, before you sleep. Here."

He put some of the crumbly, sticky cubes between his father's lips. The slack lips opened on bright teeth in pink plastic gums. The tongue slowly swept the dates into his mouth. The muscles in the jaws tightened and moved beneath the shiny skin. The mouth opened and closed as the tongue moved the mash about among the teeth.

"Tamar," he said. "My daughter."

3.

"Gratitude," said Ayelet.

"For what?" Danny wanted to know.

"For marrying me. I was twenty, crippled, the army wouldn't even accept me as a volunteer, and all my friends were gone, dead in the car crash or dead in the army. It was just after the Six Day War and I was alone. And I was frightened that I would always be alone, that I would never ...."

"Never what?"

"Marry. Like Hedva. Have a home and a family."

"Like Hedva."

"Like Hedva. Live a normal life."

They sat at the little table in the kitchen. The morning light subtly washed and ebbed in the room as the breeze moved the curtains on the window above their heads. Together they were hollowing out what remained of the Sabbath challah, picking at crumbs.

"Does gratitude go on forever?" Danny asked. "Does it never change?"

"We married and you were born right away," she said. "I was grateful for my life."

Even a little before my time, thought Danny.

"You filled my life with joy and love. I never knew there could be such love."

"We were talking about Nimrod."

"Gratitude turns into a comfortable habit," his mother continued. "Oh, we had our rough times, like any other couple, but we have had a good life together. I'm very grateful to your father."

"But did you love him?"

"He's a good man. He's always been a good man to me. He

helped me when I needed him."

Danny thought of Hedva. Tamar was twenty-three. While Ayelet was grateful, Nimrod celebrated a quarter-century of infidelity.

"Your father is dying of cancer in the next room," she said. "How can you even ...." She would have gone on, but her voice caught, and she wiped her eyes with a corner of the dishrag.

Danny watched her, his silent hands on the table before him. What did his father have that commanded such loyalty? Or what did his mother lack and need? Someone to fulfill her tepid dream of marriage and family, her trim ideal of the ordinary. Did she realize with what predictable inevitability her dream satisfied the norm? A straying husband sleeping with the friend who betrayed her. Ayelet was constantly deceived by those who claim to love her.

No, Danny decided, she did not realize. She could not realize. He knew his mother. Her physical incapacity reflected a spiritual lameness. Perhaps insight had been removed with her leg below the knee. Her dreams were so commonplace and unimaginative. They reflected the limitations of her mind that looked at the world with eyes formed and fixed more than forty years ago.

Did Nimrod and Ayelet ever love? Did they ever touch each other's bodies with tenderness? He could not imagine Nimrod ever kissing his mother's reddened stub, tender from the stiff plastic prosthesis. Nor could he easily imagine his father rutting after his neighbor's wife, the blond woman not yet decayed, and the decaying man not yet dead.

Dead and decayed. Like Hedva's husband, Ernu. When Tami was two, Hedva's husband died somewhere along the canal in the War of Attrition. He existed now only in the fading marriage photograph that looked down upon Hedva's busy bed. Was the source of Ernu's wry smile, frozen forever, his comic awareness of the glandular drive of the wife he held in his fading arms? Or was his mouth awry in the sadder knowledge that his daughter carried no genes of his? Ernu the Watcher. Ernu the Recipient. Hunkered in a bunker. Banal beside the canal. Catching bombs until one caught him. That's Ernu all over. Dead then. Decayed now.

Unlike the dying Nimrod who decays before he dies. Nimrod of the Nimble Rod, the hunter with a head for Hedva. And golden Hedva egregiously grieving. Would she grieve more for the father of her daughter than she did for the husband she deceived, who was then a boy barely twenty?

And then Nimrod didn't die. The door at the end of the hall slowly opened one evening and he appeared in the doorway. His two triple-pronged canes arced slowly forward. His legs moved, dark and indistinct beneath the thin fabric of his nightgown. His cancer, like his sins, had slipped into remission.

Ayelet rose to help him, but Nimrod waved her away. She cleared a place for him at the table, but Nimrod stood on the cold tiles in the harsh kitchen light, his pink, naked feet, scabby with white curls of flaking skin. The light scintillating in the tarnished silver stubble on his face.

And then he was alive.

Danny came home one evening from the army and found him eating cake in the kitchen. Hedva sat beside him. Two cups of tea. Two plates. His mother stood with her back to the counter, holding cup and saucer, and smiling at her son's homecoming.

"Danny!" she said. "How good!"

"I've got ten days," he said. He reached for the telephone, dialed, and said, "Danny Benzion. I'm at my parents' house. Yes, that's the number."

"Are you hungry, Danny?" Ayelet asked. "Have some cake. It's delicious. Hedva made it."

"No, thank you, mom. Is Tami home?" he asked Hedva--and then he was suddenly embarrassed by the cruelty of the question.

Hedva swiveled in the chair, her golden hair bouncing about her rosy, smiling, upturned face. What was it? Danny thought. What was there about Nimrod in his late forties that attracted a young married woman--still golden more than two decades later--to betray her new husband and take for her lover a man twice her age and married to her best friend?

Danny knew stories of his father's life almost too rich to believe. Survival, vengeance, triumph, immigration, marriage, family--and now mistress, daughter. But Danny knew nothing of his father's life. Whom did he love? What did he feel when he killed to avenge the deaths of his first wife and children? It could not be what Danny felt. Danny saw, as from a great distance, the faces of Abu Jihad's wife and daughter as they stood in the widening pool of the man's blood.

Danny realized he was merely acquainted with this old man, this merchant of death, transporter of pilfered property, incendiary. He did not know his own father. What blue energy lay beneath Nimrod's translucent skin? What midnight fire powered his heart?

"Yes," said Hedva. "She was going to take a shower and lie down for a while. But you can go in. She should be up by now. The door's open."

4.

The door to the apartment was open. The door to Hedva's bedroom was open, too, and Danny looked in upon the neatly made bed, puffed pillows, photograph of Ernu, the dead and deceived husband--a boy then not as old as Danny was now--with his arms around his wife. He immediately compared it to the room where Nimrod once lay dying. A rumpled bed, crushed pillows, and no pictures at all. How neatened the lives of women were.

The door to Tamar's room was closed. He tapped lightly, dipped the handle, and pushed it open upon her disarray. The doors of her closet were ajar, the drawers of her dresser were open to various lengths, her clothes were draped on surfaces or piled beside her kitbag on the floor. She was asleep, but she turned toward him as he stood in the door and opened her eyes to him.

"You're not my mother," she said.

"No," he said.

"Where is she?"

"Over there."

Tamar radiated the heat of her sleep. Her skin was smooth, the muscles of her face slack, not yet animated by the rigors of being awake. The thin sheet draped along her body gave her the elegance of Greek marble. Only her loose heavy hair was modern.

"How's Nimrod today?" she asked.

"Much better. He gets stronger every day."

"Just when you thought you would lose him."

"Yes. He continues to amaze me."

"Did I ever tell you that I envied you?"

"No," said Danny. "What for?"

"I know more about your father than I know about my own."

Danny paused before he said, "Ernu died when you were a baby. How could you know anything about him?"

"He survived that horrible car accident, he survived the Six Day War, and then he died in the peace."

"Surely Hedva must have said something. After all, they were in the accident together, and he didn't die until later."

"Yes, they were in the accident, but they weren't together."

"What do you mean?" said Danny.

"They were with other people. I used to think your mother was with my father, but maybe I'm wrong. Anyway, Hedva and Ernu didn't fall in love until after the accident. I think it was while they were going to visit Ayelet in the hospital."

"If that's all you know about Ernu," said Danny, "he sounds like a nice guy who had good luck in the accident and then he had bad luck at the canal."

"Oh, he had red hair and freckles and a crooked smile, but he didn't kill Nazis in Argentina or travel or anything. He graduated high school and went into the army. He was twenty-two or three when he died."

Danny sat in silence, a colorless figure in the darkened room.

"I didn't know he was a red-head," he said. "The only picture I've seen is the black-and-white in your mother's room."

"Hedva always said he was not as red as you," Tamar said.

No, Danny thought, not as red as me.

And then his heart rose in his throat in wonder at his mother's daring. Lying in a hospital bed with a severed leg and alive with Ernu's child, did she see her two best friends fall in love even as they came to visit her? She would have measured Ernu's distress at her infirmity. She would have neglected to tell him who he was and what she knew. She would not confront him. No. That was not her way. She designed her life to serve and to survive. So Danny was his mother's son after all and amazed at her courage.

His eyes filled with tears for the fathers he never knew, for the philandering hero he loved who was not his father and for the ignorant, unlucky hero Danny didn't know but who was. Nimrod, the silent avenger who married the little lame girl old enough to be his daughter and who must already then have been round with Ernu's child; Nimrod, who cheated death by nesting a woman and founding a family and giving a name to a boy who wasn't his but who grew up to be him. And then finding solace for his gain beyond retribution for his loss with the golden neighbor whose husband, Ernu--whether either of them knew it or not--was the father of Nimrod's own son. And Nimrod, giving his son's father a child to raise as his own--a daughter to Ernu, the Uninformed, the red-headed soldier who waited by the canal for his death to find him.

Danny's eyes brimmed in despair at the impossibility of unfolding the complications of his parents' love, the sinuous obligations of their sophisticated fidelities.

Tamar saw his eyes brim and opened her arms to him.

Sheep's Clothing

Then come home my children...

"And then this voice said...."

"What kind of voice?"

"American. He said he wanted to invite us to dinner at the Casbah on Yirmiahu in North Tel Aviv. Shani, do you know it?"

"Very nice and very expensive. Yariv and I haven't been there in years."

"Well, you're invited too."

"But, D'vorah, what's it all about?"

"I don't know! He said he was the husband of a friend of ours from Mayan Zwi. We hadn't seen each other since 1958 and this was going to be a surprise for her too. They were in Israel just for a few days on their way to Turkey. This friend of ours had spoken about us for years and years because we were her best friends in school."

"What's her name?"

"Wouldn't say."

"We have a best friend without a name? Does he have a name at least?"

"Gordon, he said."

"Gordon what?"

"Wouldn't say."

The telephone line between them was silent until Shani said, "D'vorah, this is all very mysterious. How does he know it's us?"

"He called the kibbutz."

"Don't say!" said Shani.

"He was speaking American, but eventually they found someone from the old days who got D'vorah from 'Bee.' But since Rose could be Vered or Shoshanna, nobody made the connection to 'Shani' so that's why he called me. He asked if I was the D'vorah who was in school at Mayan Zwi maybe thirty years ago and was my best friend called Rose and if I was and if you were would I please come to dinner, all expenses paid, and would I call you and invite you and so I'm calling you and inviting you."

"I don't believe it!" said Shani.

But D'vorah wanted to know: "Are we going?"

"Oh yes, I wouldn't miss this for the world. I'm eager to find out who my best friend was."

"Will your mother-in-law let you go out?"

"Oh, I'll get a baby-sitter for her. Or a nurse. Or Yariv can stay home and sit with her."

"She recognizes him?"

"Most of the time she thinks he's his father and talks to him about his brother--I mean, his father's brother--you know, the one killed in '48. I think she was in love with him. That's why Yariv was named after him. It's all very confusing because sometimes she slips into the present and I never know whether she's talking about adultery or incest. Yariv can't tell the difference, but since he brought her here, he spends even less time at home than he did before ."

The line was again silent for a moment. And then D'vorah asked, "Business or girl friends?"

"Yes," said Shani.

"Do you know who it is?"

"No, I don't."

"Do you have any suspicions?"

"I don't care."

"You're not interested?"

"It's not important."

"Divorce him," said D'vorah, not for the first time.

"I can't do that," Shani responded. "We need each other. We

give each other legitimacy."

"It must be very hard for you."

"Nothing lasts forever," said Shani. "How's Elimelech?"

"Oh, healing nicely, thanks. He's got eight more days of leave and then he has to return to his unit."

"Lucky boy."

"Luckier mother. It was only a flesh wound. He'll have an interesting scar on his thigh that will be fascinating to the predatory girls he's eager to meet."

"Did we ever used to be predatory girls?" Shani teased.

"No," said D'vorah. "Only one of us."

"Whatever happened?"

"We grew up," laughed D'vorah.

"Shall I come to you or will you come to me?"

"Let Yariv drive," D'vorah said. "You guys can pick me up on the way in."

"You don't mind being squeezed in the back?" Shani asked.

"No. And it will give him a chance to show off his car."

"This is going to be great," Shani said.

2.

> *... the sun is gone down*
> *And the dews of night arise*

The red Mercedes convertible turned off the coast road in the pearly evening and headed toward the sea at Tel Baruch where the bracing sea air is sometimes delicately perfumed with excrement, and the lilting girls, who stand in pairs beside the road in micro-miniskirts, are sometimes female.

Yariv wheeled the two-seater toward the city, past the beach where Patriot batteries had tilted toward the sky like unloading dump-trucks. He passed the tiny, silent airport and turned again toward the sea and the Reading Power Station whose unique contribution to Tel Aviv they had seen from five miles away as a yellow-brown smudge on the evening.

Instead of crossing the modern concrete bridge arching over the fetid Yarkon, the Mercedes slipped off the highway through an embankment, among the bushes, and along cracked tarmac toward the one-lane condemned bridge. Weakened by internal stress, girder and iron truss were held by bracing bars and rivets that bled red rust beneath black paint.

When they spilled out onto Ussishkin between the fusty, fragrant river-park and the peccant city, they drove along the darkened narrow street toward the lights around the Peer Cinema. The car twisted left then right and found a place to park on Yirmiahu. D'vorah extricated herself with difficulty from the little jump-seat behind the driver.

"This is it," said Shani before the buff building with the bottle-bottoms set in the wall.

"Looks just like a casbah," said Yariv. D'vorah punched him playfully on the arm.

"Three for dinner?" asked the maitre d'.

"No. We're meeting Gordon Somebody," said Yariv, taking charge.

"This way, please." He led them among the tables, up two steps, and along the bar to a round booth set among plastic plants in subdued light.

A dapper gentleman rose to meet them. He wore a trim summer suit perfectly tailored with a Windsor knot in a rose foulard above a creamy shirt. His eyes were blue as Dutch porcelain, his black hair was eloquently barbered, his tan was expensive and so was his scent. Yariv estimated his income as seven figures.

"I'm so glad you could come," he said, extending an elegant hand.

"What is it, Gordon?" said a voice from the dark bend of the table.

"I wanted to surprise you, Limor. I've asked your friends, Bea and Rose, to join us. And you are?"

"Yariv. And I'm very pleased to meet you, Gordon. I'm married to Shani."

As D'vorah and Shani peered around the edge of the booth, they saw in the shadow a pale woman with coifed silver hair. She wore a blue chiffon blouse that rose in a column and broke into a flounce beneath her chin.

"Limor! Is it really you?" Shani exclaimed.

The two women slipped into the booth beside her and the three of them chattered with incandescent vivacity in Hebrew while the men sat on the aisle, Gordon in adoration, Yariv with increasing disinterest.

"What do you do exactly?" Yariv asked at last.

"What? Me? Oh, I fabricate steel," Gordon answered, surprised to be called away.

"Where?" Yariv continued.

"Shreveport."

"Where's that?"

"Louisiana."

"Where's that in relation to New York?"

"About seventeen hundred miles to the southwest."

"Oh. Near Los Angeles."

"Closer to New Orleans, actually," said Gordon. And then he said, "You know, I'm really glad I could bring her here and surprise her like this. We're on our way to set up a milling plant at Diyarfakir in eastern Turkey. She didn't want to come to Israel. No. But when we changed planes in Athens, we got on the plane to Tel Aviv instead of the one to Ankara and she never noticed until we landed here."

"However did you do that?" Yariv asked. "I could never trick Shani like that."

"It's easy to fool someone who knows that you love her," Gordon said.

"So I don't get it. Why did you come to Israel instead of Turkey?"

"You know, she's been talking about--what are their Hebrew

names, Beatrice and Rose?"

"Bee is D'vorah and Rose is Shoshanna. Shani."

"Limor has been talking about them for years. Best friends. Out of touch all this time. Sustained her when she arrived here from the camp. It seemed to me that these people should get together again. Limor resisted it. So much had intervened, you see. But when I think something's right, I do it. I convinced her to come on this trip to Turkey, and the switch in the airport was easy."

"I know something about the steel business," Yariv offered.

"She was ... pleased, yes, pleased that we came. And it makes me so happy to be able to make her happy. A girl like that. She was born in the camps, you know. Came here in '50, and her mother, who was dying even then, took her to the States in '58. That was the year she was separated from ...? "

"D'vorah and Shani."

"Yes. She must have been about thirteen or fourteen then. Grew up in the States but she was haunted, yes haunted by the past, by the horrors of her infancy, a shattered childhood, and then the death of her mother. Deprived of everything that we take as the basic decencies of youth. And I," said Gordon, "who grew up safe in the States, buffered from that experience that separated her from all normal life--I've done everything I can to make up for what she's lost."

Gordon looked at the pale woman talking in the corner.

"Do you plan on doing any business in Israel?" Yariv persisted.

"The important thing was to reestablish contact, don't you see? To show her that the happy years she spent in school with D'vorah and Shani were not lost. I think I've heard about every day they spent together. Climbing in the hills, swimming in the fishponds at Mayan Zwi, getting lost in the cave, fighting with the kids from Ma'agen Mi'cha-el, being attacked by the Arabs from Fureidis. Terrifying. That woman suffered more in her childhood than most people suffer in a lifetime."

After a while, bored by the suffering of women, Yariv said, "Are we going to eat?"

Choosing from the splendid French menu, the carnivores ordered flesh. The more delicate women ordered shark.

When the bones were picked clean and cleared away and the coffee cups soiled by lipstick, D'vorah and Shani slid across the seats toward the aisle. But as Limor started to move, the plastic flowers on the shelf behind caught her hair. As she lifted her hand to disentangle herself, the sleeve of her blouse fell back from her wrist to reveal the delicate tracery of pale blue numbers--the capital letter A followed by a three, a one, a nine, and a seven--raggedly tattooed on the inside of her left forearm.

"Oh, here, let me help," said Gordon kneeling on the booth and reaching in to free her hair as her arm fell back beneath the table and into her lap.

3.

Your spring and your day are wasted in play

"Goodbye."

"Goodbye."

"We must keep in touch now."

"We will. We will. Goodbye."

"Goodbye."

The heavy door closed on silence, and the happy faces, raised arms, and fluttering hands disappeared as the Mercedes moved off into Yirmiahu, turned right onto Diezengoff, and headed out of town.

Shani turned in her seat to look at D'vorah and both women started to laugh.

"If he hadn't said 'Limor,' I would never have known who she was," Shani said.

"Limor? Who Limor? What Limor?" Yariv was mystified.

"Who ever knew her last name? She was Limor from Ma'agan

Mi'cha-el."

"She must have been in class with us," said D'vorah, "but I don't remember her at all."

"And the stories she told. Did you remember climbing in the Carmel?" Shani asked.

"We took a field trip to the Ca'ananite caves around that time. But it was the three kibbutzim together."

As they passed the elegantly architectured mortuary where the dead from Tel Aviv are brought and washed and dressed for the grave, displayed in a shroud, and subjected to praise and prayer before being trucked to the cemetery, Yariv said, "And the three of you swimming in the fish ponds."

"Don't be stupid, Yariv," said Shani. "There weren't any fish ponds at Mayan Zwi or at Ma'agen Mi'cha-el either in those days."

"And when there were fish ponds," said D'vorah, "no one in their right mind would ever go swimming in all that fish slime. Ugh."

"I don't get it," said Yariv. "You mean, she made it all up?"

"She was never a friend of ours while we were in school," said D'vorah. "We were a closed society."

"Well," he said expansively, "I think you ought to be flattered. Here's someone who thought so much of you as a child--loved you or envied you--that she made up this story about being friends with you. It's a harmless enough deception."

"It's sick," said Shani.

"One doesn't expect perfect health from a holocaust survivor," he said.

"Holocaust survivor? Nonsense," said Shani. "Her mother may have been the kibbutz whore for all I know, but Limor was born at Ma'agen Mi'cha-el."

"But didn't a holocaust survivor come to the kibbutz about that time, Shani? What was her name? Goldy?"

"Yes, Goldene," said Shani. "We called her 'Zahava.'"

"'Zahava,' right!" D'vorah laughed, remembering. "She was

great, a wonderful, funny girl who would do anything. Remember when they were stuffing dead birds to make a museum for the kibbutz, and she caught an egret?"

D'vorah and Shani laughed at the memory of the frightened hungry bird knocking over the display of stuffed birds in the museum.

"But Limor was a holocaust survivor," Yariv insisted. "I saw the numbers tattooed on her arm."

"What a clever deception," said Shani. "She never had them as a child. We would have known. We would have seen them every day. Everyone would have known."

"Maybe because you saw them every day," said Yariv, "they became ordinary for you and you've forgotten."

"That's like Waldheim forgetting he was a Nazi," D'vorah said.

"But why would she want to have numbers tattooed on her arm so she could pass as a holocaust survivor?" he asked.

They drove in silence.

Then Shani said, "Maybe she did it herself with ink and a needle."

"Well, it got her a husband who adores her," said D'vorah.

"I've never seen anything like it," Shani enthused. "But he's an American. They're like that. Oh, D'vorah, why couldn't we have married soft, adoring American men?"

"If what you say is true," said Yariv, "and I don't believe it for a minute, then I feel sorry for Gordon. He's the one who's been tricked."

"Well," said Shani, "the husband's always the last to know."

Yariv drove easily with his right hand on the power steering. His left hand lay on his thigh. It slipped down along the side of his seat. He reached behind him in the dark until he felt the fabric of D'vorah's skirt. He rubbed his backward hand along her bony ankle, her muscled gam, her warm underthigh. She hugged his dark hand with her dark knees as the car turned away from the beach toward the coast road.

4.

And your winter and night in disguise.
                                    --William Blake

"The nice thing about Gordon," said Shani as she hung up her thin, spring frock of pale yellow wool, "is that he is so attentive to her. A woman appreciates that."

"What?" said Yariv.

She didn't answer. Standing between the light on the dresser and the light on the bedside table to give him a three-quarters front view, she unhooked her bra and took it off. She stepped into the bathroom, heels clicking against the floor tiles. When she returned, she stepped down out of her shoes.

"The clever thing about Limor," she said, "is that she has manufactured a history that occupies her husband's imagination. She really doesn't exist. He's not attentive to her but to some person she created, someone he imagines."

"Oh, if what you say is true, she's a fraud all right. I pity the poor husband."

"Rich husbands are never to be pitied," Shani said evenly. "They all get what they deserve. And what they don't deserve, they buy."

"He's mega-bucks," Yariv continued. "I tried to tap into that, but he wasn't biting."

"You tried to work a deal?"

"Look, Shani, we had to talk about something while you hens were squawking. We talked business. I admire a man who makes money."

"Is that what you found most to admire about Gordon?"

"I know what I like, and I liked what I saw."

She sat on the edge of the bed and twisted around toward him, her pendant breasts moving in the subdued light of the bedroom.

"Do you like what you see now?" she asked.

"Always," he said, his sex rising.

"Not for sale," she said turning away.

She turned off the light and settled back among the pillows. Night noises from the street and pinpricks of light invaded the room.

After a while, she said in a small night voice, "Do you know what ... I'm ... doing ... now? I'm thinking of Gordon. I'm imagining his tongue licking me all over. I feel his breath and his lips and his tongue playing with my nipples. I'm thinking of Gordon's warm mouth on my vagina and I'm feeling good, feeling good, going all warm and liquid inside. Feeling good."

"Let me help you," he said thickly.

"Go fuck your whores," she bristled.

In the morning he was gone about the busy business of making money. She found his coffee cup beside the morning paper on the breakfast table.

She looked in on her mother-in-law. Handling her flesh was like handling loose cake dough, but Shani finally manipulated her into a dressing gown and propped her up--evacuated, washed, fed, and asleep--in a wheelchair by the open bedroom window. The sheers billowed as the sweet colors of spring scented the room. Jonquil, frizia, amnon-and-tamar, nasturtium.

When D'vorah came, they sat in the bright living room overlooking the garden.

"I can't get over Limor," D'vorah said. "I can't imagine anyone going to those extremes."

"I don't think she created anything so extreme," said Shani. "What interests me is what she was hiding. No, the deception is explicable: she wanted to be more fascinating than a ditch-water kibbutz girl. She wanted a history and a pain that people could recognize and sympathize with."

"Then she's no different from the rest of us," said D'vorah. "We all create the little histories and deceptions by which we live."

"Yes" said Shani. "It's an act of protective selfishness and really quite understandable. But the more interesting question for me is who was she? Why did she feel so bad about herself, so guilty or lonely, that she had to become someone else in order to endure who she was?"

"Don't we all do that, too?"

"Yes," said Shani, smiling wanly at D'vorah. "But not everyone feels that being a holocaust survivor is better than who she is. Not everybody feels so bad ... that ... she ...."

"Do you feel bad about yourself, Shani?"

But Shani was looking down, and D'vorah couldn't see her moist eyes.

"Do me," she whispered, not looking up.

"You have to speak more clearly," said D'vorah who heard what she said.

"Do me, please."

D'vorah moved to the couch and put her arms about Shani's shoulders.

"You have to say you want me to do you," she said.

"I want to feel good," Shani said. "Help me feel good. Make me feel good."

"There, there," murmured D'vorah, gathering her into her arms, stroking her hair, stroking her hair and the back of her neck, stroking her back, gently, gently laying her back upon the couch.

The Brown Boys

Hebron is in another country, closer to Teheran than to Tel Aviv. The brown houses root in the brown soil and hunker down upon the earth with the fanatic attachment of a squinting peasant haunching his heels. In Hebron, Amnon photographed an abstract expressionist world, a composition in brown rectangles irregularly alternating with shadowed black squares and walls white or startling blue in the shimmering sun. Rising throughout the town and along the horizon, white minarets point at heaven. Amnon photographed them as rockets with divine warheads.

Sometimes Amnon longed for a splash of red and the tinkle of neon to break the brown monotony of Hebron. He and the other reservists were there to protect Rabbi Levinger and his disciples, risky cowboys who thrust themselves into the very dangerous heart of Hebron from which Jews had been expelled with slaughter in 1939. Irritated by grit and light, Amnon's platoon lingered on street corners, watched from rooftops, as alert as the weather would allow.

They had to be alert because Hebron is unpredictable. Suddenly the brown boys appear in a crowd, faces wrapped, stones in hand. One warm day, when Amnon was stationed at the gate to Beit Hadassah, a slim brown girl took a knife from her sleeve and stuck it in Itzik's back; he turned and shot her dead. Yes, the brown boredom of Hebron was dangerous.

Otherwise, Amnon liked reserve duty. Though like everyone else he complained about the interruption to his ordinary life when he received the call-up, Amnon was secretly pleased and looked forward to gathering with the boys again. Old friends resurrected in an hour the familiar patterns of speech and behavior they hadn't used for the year they were apart. The company settled into the old routines they performed comfortably together. The regularity of army life appealed to him: six hours on, six hours off; seven to one, one to seven; every day and every night for forty-five days every year.

The photographs showed that reserve duty rendered the fat from his body, browned his skin, taught him to live with privation. The six hours off were really five, and once they returned to the base and showered and slept there was hardly any time to eat. He was never hungry in Hebron. Army food was impossible to eat on rooftops. Chocolate melted in the summer. Sandwiches dried out. Apples were hot. He returned from reserve service thin from lack of food, fit from physical activity, brown from the sun, and full of jokes and stories, games and tricks, the spiritual enrichment of army life.

Reserve duty was the appropriate adversative to his job at the Diaspora Museum where he sat in a large silent room and coded unidentified photographs. They came by the box-full. Every picture had a country. Every country had a synagogue and a cemetery. He liked reading tombstones in cemeteries long since destroyed and then entering the information into the computer. Reading photographs was foreign travel without the inconvenience.

Sometimes it took three weeks for his Hebron tan to fade and for him to return to the rhythms of Tel Aviv, to the coffee and cake in the afternoons after work, to the cinema in the evenings. That's what he missed most on reserve duty: the cake and the cinema. If it were not for reserve duty, Amnon could stay at home in his quiet apartment with his comfortable wife.

2.

As he sat at his dinner, Amnon heard her key scratching at the front door. Ahuva, already dressed and brushed, came through the opening into the kitchen.

"Well, hello, Mr. Braun," she said. "So nice to have you home again."

"And hello, Mrs. Braun. It's nice to be here." He stood up and hugged her. He sat down again as she put her packages on the kitchen counter.

"Guess what," she said, not looking at him. "Nadav is coming."

"Oh, for God's sake." Amnon put down his fork.

"He called me at work."

"Ahuva, I just got home from the army. I haven't even changed my clothes. I'm eating my dinner. I'm not going to the airport."

"My sister said she would be glad to pick him up."

"Birds of a feather. Damn it. He's not going to spoil my first night home."

Nadav always came suddenly, stomping into Amnon's life in mountain-walking shoes and ratty army coat, wild hair bound up with a bandanna or Indian beads, knapsack full of the trash from some distant bazaar. He was always full of stories and lies and lice.

"Do we have any Scabicin solution in the house?" Amnon asked petulantly. "He's going to need it."

How depressing. How vexing and depressing to be reminded of his worthless brother. At twenty-eight, Nadav was still on vacation, wandering the world with a knapsack, permanently tanned like some eager soldier just released from the army. He hitch-hiked, sailed, drove, rode in trains, in buses, on horseback, on dung-carts, in airplanes, walked from one pointless paradise to another, eating the food and drinking the water. He was dehydrated in Tucumcari, diarrhetic in Valparaiso. He fed chicken bones to the rats in a white public square in Calcutta and slept on the streets. A mahogany beggar fed him. He played basketball with Zoroastrians in Goa.

What a pointless, ramshackle existence, Amnon thought.

Nadav always managed to work an odd job for a week or two. Nothing permanent. Nothing with a future. He gathered enough money to go from one place to the other, but he lived no where, he owned nothing. And every year or two he would come home and rattle their lives and then be off to HaGoshrim or Neve Ur where he'd share a dreary little room with a skinny girl with long hair or, worse, he'd camp in Shalhevet's apartment, two floors below.

He'd call them a month later to say he'd made fourteen thousand dollars on that last trip and he had been in Israel long enough and so he was going to Uruguay where his friend managed a rice farm and did Amnon have anything he wanted smuggled into South America? But a few weeks later an air-letter would come from Kyoto telling them that the first plane out of Cairo was going the other way and they could write to him c/o the Israeli Embassy, Singapore, until August and that in Kuala Lampur he'd met a Brazilian girl who sold tickets for Avianca in Rangoon and that she'd managed to get him a first-class ticket gratis from Bangkok to Katmandu where he would be until November and then they were going on her vacation to the Great Barrier Reef at Darwin and maybe on to Hobart and that he didn't think he was going to Uruguay after all but that he'd tell them all about it later.

Then suddenly Nadav would call from Ben Gurion to say he was coming over. What a pointless, meaningless life. Amnon was depressed.

A sudden pounding on the hollow front door made Ahuva say "Oh!" and clutch her throat. Screams at the door and pounding. Amnon finally distinguished the cries.

"Juden 'raus! Juden 'raus!"

And then he recognized Nadav's German voice and Shalhevet's annoying giggle.

"God damn it," he said.

"Juden 'raus and into the trucks!"

"Oh, it's only Nadav," said Ahuva. But before she could get to the door, Shalhevet opened with her key and the two came bang-bumping into the kitchen while behind them somewhere a picture fell to the floor.

"Whoops," said Nadav, turning to look, his backpack slapping an upper cupboard door.

"Whoops again. Hey Amnon, I seem to have broken a picture. You ought to keep those things in a drawer where they're safe. Put it on the bill, boy. How are ya? Any *Juden* in here?"

Nadav lifted the corner of a dish towel and peered beneath.

"No *Juden* here," he said.

For some reason, Shalhevet collapsed laughing against the wall.

"Lucky thing for you, Amnon. They shoot people who hide *Juden.* Rat-tat-tat-tat-tat."

He machine-gunned around the room until he came to Ahuva.

"Baby!" he said and held his arms wide to hug her.

"Ugh, your beard is scratchy."

"Beard? Do I have a beard? It's really a disguise to get me through Customs. See, it comes off." He put a fist around his beard and lifted.

"Oh God," he cried in despair, "it's grown into my skin! I'm trapped in a beard forever. But look, girl, it's your rich uncle Nadav returned from the wilds of merry India!"

He danced a jig and slapped his thighs and arms and rolled his eyes and stamped his feet and toppled and juggled and mewed and barked and barking pawed and pawing licked and finally with a whistle and a scream pulled a gorgeous orange and lavender cloth bordered in shimmering green gold and blue-gold that billowed and bowed and seemed to fill the room.

Ahuva and Shalhevet squeaked in delight.

"Ohhh, it's beautiful," they said.

"Well, come and see what else I got for you."

"Oooo, presents."

Nadav swung the backpack from his shoulders and almost fell over his khaki duffel on the floor as Shalhevet sprang to catch him screaming, but he caught his balance by stomping one foot so hard on the floor and slamming up against the cabinet that he rattled every dish on the table.

"In the living room, for God's sake," said Amnon. "Take all your junk in there."

With much pounding and stamping, the backpack and duffel were dragged to the living room and surrounded by Shalhevet and Ahuva giggling.

Amnon looked at the chaos in the kitchen. As he put down his fork, he chipped the plate. He looked at the petal of pottery, picked it up, intensely aware suddenly of the smooth glaze on one side, the rough unglaze on the other. He left it, with his napkin, in the gravy on his plate and went to take a shower.

Drying the folds of his flesh, Amnon heard the squeaks of delight the girls gave the trash his brother unfolded from the backpack and duffel. He scrubbed his arms and legs with the rough towel to get the dust of Hebron off his skin. He dried his back, carefully avoiding the hairy mole behind his heart. He shaved and dressed. He remembered Trevor Howard saying in some old film about India that one must always maintain one's dignity in the presence of the barbarians. His back was straight, his shoulders square as he turned out of the bedroom and entered the living room of giggles and squeals.

He stepped into an oriental bazaar. The room was disoriented by color, brilliant and violent oranges, golds, greens, reds, blues, batik and tie-dyed silks, cottons, feathery wools draped from the light fixture, the pictures, the mirrors, across the chairs, tables, lamps, sofa, on the floor, the walls. On the coffee table was spread a rich mound of silver and semi-precious stones: new silver rings, dark silver bracelets, necklaces, slave anklets and armlets with bells, rings for the ear and the hand and the nose and the toe, belt buckles, brooches, pins and pendants, curious, ornate, curved and carved and crafted.

Nadav stood in the center of the room beside the disemboweled duffel.

"And what do you think of this, my pretties?"

He pulled a gorgeous, diaphanous dress of blue-orange silk

batik from the bag and shook it out in a slow graceful bow like a sheet in a summer breeze and held it up on one side and held it on the other and cast it away left-handedly. It fell across the wedding-portrait on the television set.

"Choose something. Take anything you want. Here Ahuva, a lovely dress, just for you. Wear it tonight.

"It's beautiful. Shalhevet, look!"

"It's just your size. What's the tag say? 38? Right. That dress is about fifteen rupees in Calcutta--oh, about two dollars, six shekels."

"Six shekels!"

"Cost me a little less."

"Six shekels, Shalhevet. Look at this. It's gorgeous."

"That's all hand embroidery."

"My God, Shalhevet. Look at this. You couldn't buy this for two hundred in HaMashbir."

"If you could find it."

"Six shekels. How does it look?"

"Here's a piece of fabric, Shalhevet, finest cotton, woven from long-hair cotton, tough, strong, thin as air." He billowed a gorgeous tie-dyed cotton at her.

"Three-and-a-half yards, enough for a summer dress, and you can make halter and panties to match."

"It's just beautiful, Nadav," Shalhevet moaned.

"Ahuva, try this fabric: seven rupees--about three shekels--it's virgin wool, but who cares about the morality of sheep? Cost me at my exchange under a dollar. Take it. Here's some more."

He filled the air with gorgeous colors.

"And who's going to clean up this mess?" asked Amnon.

"Ohh, Amnon, look at this. Isn't it beautiful? Doesn't it make you want to cry it's so beautiful?"

"I want to cry when I think that someone," Amnon was looking at Nadav, "is going to have to fold up all this stuff and put it back in the bag."

"See this dress, Amnon? All hand embroidered. Think of the

time and effort it took to do this. And it only costs six shekels. I can't believe it. Ohhh, isn't it just too beautiful?"

Amnon sniffed loudly and crinkled his nose.

"What's that funny smell?" he asked.

"They use kerosene in the batik process, especially on silk," said Nadav.

"The place smells like the Reading Power Station. Or Haifa."

"The kerosene smell hangs out in a day or two."

"My God, it smells like Haifa in here," said Amnon sourly.

"Turn on a fan."

"Listen, Nadav, I'm sorry we can't stay and talk tonight, but I just got back from the army ...."

"Where were you?"

"Hebron .... And on my first night back we always go to a movie. It's like a tradition."

"What are you going to see?"

"You wouldn't know. It's a double feature at the Cinematech, actually. A black-and-white Akira Kurasawa film made in 1954, *The Seven Samurai.* In 1960 Hollywood set the same story in the old West, called it *The Magnificent Seven,* and filmed it in technicolor. It has, let me see, Yul Brenner, Steve McQueen, James Coburn in a great role, Robert Vaughn, Charles Bronson, and what's his name, Eli Wallach, plays the Mexican bandit chief."

"If you know so much about it, why are you going to see it?"

"It's his favorite film," said Ahuva. "He even saw it on our honeymoon."

"No," said Shalhevet.

"I like that film, both films, actually, but I've never seen them together on the same bill."

"I honestly don't remember the last movie I saw," Nadav said, his hands in the bowels of the duffel bag. "Someplace in India, I think. It was an experience."

"Well, I certainly don't want to miss anything. C'mon, Ahuva. Are you staying here tonight?" Amnon asked Nadav.

"Shalhevet invited me."

"Fine. Open the windows when you leave."

The door closed on silence. A few corners of silk batik waved a gorgeous good-bye and fell silent. Shalhevet smiled. Nadav smiled and said, "If I sit down now, I'll fall asleep. Then you'll have to fold up all this merchandise yourself."

"I don't mind."

"Thank you, but I'm not that tired."

Nadav swept the silver from the coffee table into the backpack and gathered a laundry of rainbows into his arms.

3.

Amnon came down the uneven stone steps to the bus stop.

"My brother the Indian silk merchant."

"Isn't it marvelous?"

"Junk!"

"Oh, no, Amnon, you didn't look at it carefully. It was beautiful."

"Junk, Ahuva. I say that stuff was junk. That silk, did you see it? My God, you could see right through it."

"It's a summer-weight fabric."

"But it's not substantial. There's no weight to it. What can you do with it? It's like him."

"I would make it into a dress."

"Not a chance. A scarf maybe, or a handkerchief, but not a dress--never. If you wore a dress like that, the rabbis would spray you with paint, set you on fire, or have you arrested for indecency. But I'll tell you one thing. I think it's a cover. I think he's peddling drugs and this import business is just a front."

"No!"

"My brother the Indian silk merchant! Don't you believe it for a moment. He doesn't earn thousands of dollars in one month--five times my salary--peddling dresses to boutiques."

They were silent for a while before she said, "But at least he looks good, don't you think, Amnon?"

"He looks terrible."

"Oh, I think he looks much better than he did when he came back from Africa that time, remember?"

"He looks emaciated. Did you see how his shirt kept coming out of his pants. He doesn't even wear a belt. Sloppy. And his beard is long and scraggly."

"It looked clean at least."

4.

How do I look?" said Shalhevet.

Nadav looked up from his half-packed duffel. Shalhevet stood in the doorway in a long dress of purple, green, gold. The halogen made the dress shimmer and shine. Her hair piled loosely atop her head emphasized her long neck, the scalloped neckline revealed her fragile shadowed collar-bone. Her feet were bare. She was iridescent.

"Beautiful," said Nadav.

"It's a little tight in the shoulders and across the bust, don't you think?"

"That's because the sleeve is square-cut, see. Western sleeves are set in. And no darts."

"It's so lovely and light."

"Here." He fastened a silver belt loosely athwart her hips and smoothed the fabric beneath it, down her flanks, along her pelvic bone.

"Let me try a slave anklet, too." She held out a delicate foot as though for a glass slipper.

She tinkled to the dress mirror in the hall and turned and twisted, hands on her hips.

"I don't like the belt," she said, "but I like the slave thing."

5.

The bus windows rattled, shimmied their reflections; their

reflections shook and shivered, forever unquiet and noisy as the bus bumped. The white blob in the black window wavered as Ahuva said,

"Do you think he'll ever settle down and get married and be as happy as we are?"

She squeezed her husband's arm.

"No. He's too selfish. He can't stand being confined. Work, wife, life in the real world would be like prison to him. He has no imaginative life into which to escape. He doesn't go to movies, can you imagine?"

"I wish he would get married, though. Some nice girl. Someone to cook for him and keep him clean. Then he wouldn't keep wandering all over the globe."

"Who would want him?"

"There are some girls who would," she said seriously. "That's what he needs. A nice girl and a home. And a steady job."

"I wouldn't hire him."

"Amnon! Your own brother?"

"I wouldn't. He'd work for two weeks and then disappear. He's a short-timer. That's his style. Here today, gone tomorrow. Always looking for some new place. I wouldn't hire him."

"A nice girl," Ahuva said. "That would settle him down. Someone like Shalhevet."

"Good--oh, that's good. Two crazies."

"Now Amnon. You know Shalhevet is a sweet girl and very sensible. I think she'd be perfect for him."

"Wonderful! I'm all for their getting married. Tonight. Then the two of them could go off to Tasmania or somewhere."

"Amnon!"

"Or Haifa--that's better--both of them, with the kerosene dresses."

6.

Nadav heard the slave bells jingle. He turned down the flap of the backpack and listened to the alternating tinkle and pad of anklet and foot. He smelled sandalwood. Light filtered through jacaranda and made the orange persimmon glow. The light brown girl with ebony eyes who spoke Tamil and smelled of jasmine. The hills above Quilon in Travancore. All India at their back and the infinite sea beneath them. He saw foot and ankle, leg, knee, and thigh before he saw the brilliant yellow-orange-violet dress.

"This is much better, don't you think?" Shalhevet said.

"Oh yes, much better."

"It's more like a shirt than a dress, cut square all around with a little slit here on the side."

"And that's the selvage, not a hem."

"Couldn't put a hem on this," Shalhevet said turning up a corner of the fabric. "It's too thin."

"And too short. Here." Nadav tugged it down. "It's a little wrinkled from traveling, but you might get another two-three centimeters once it's ironed."

"It's very short as a dress."

"Let me take these bells off. They take the eye away from the line of your leg."

Her mauve panties showed at the slit in the side.

"Your panties are showing."

"Yes. I'll have to wear a bikini. It's better as a shirt."

"Or none at all."

"It's still a little tight in the bust."

"Try it without a bra," Nadav said.

7.

"Here we are," said Amnon. "I love Tel Aviv. It's the other end of the world from the dust of Hebron. Just smell the air. Sometimes I think that Carlebach and Ibn Gvirol are my spiritual home. Don't you?"

"I like North Tel Aviv better."

"Oh, you're just a stick in the mud. Look at the lights, the excitement." She looked. He looked.

"I'm up today," Amnon said. "I'm back from reserve duty. I've forgotten all about my stupid brother. I'm in the greatest town in the world with the greatest gal in the world. And I'm going to see the world's greatest films."

8.

"That's much better," said Nadav, leaning back on the duffel.

"Do you like?"

"Yes. I do. A lot."

She smiled and turned to the mirror.

"You've put away everything," she said.

"And now it's time to put my body into bed."

"That's my job," she said.

"But I'm not done yet."

"What?"

"There's one more dress to put away," said Nadav.

"Oh," she smiled. She took it off.

She lit a candle in the bedroom. The sheets were cool, her body burning.

"Shal-hev-et. Shal-hev-et," he said.

She laughed and opened her arms as he lay down in her heat.

"What did you think when you heard I was coming?" he said as he kissed her chin and her throat, his brown beard making her hot skin shine.

"And what do you think now," he said, kissing her nipples into a pretty shrinking.

"And here?"

His mouth was wandering down her sun-browned body, kissing and caressing.

"And now?"

She smiled.

"And what do you think now?" he said.

"And here?"

"And here?"

"And now?"

His mouth and warm breath were busy with her body.

"Oh," she said.

And then she said, "Ohhh."

His beard was moist. The dampness tickled her chin.

"Is it incest for me to sleep with my brother's wife's sister?" he asked.

"I hope so," she said. "And often."

Then Horst Buchholst rode down the dusty hillside and dismounted. He unstrapped his pistol while the shy brown girl smiled to herself. Steve McQueen and Yul Brenner urged their horses crisply over the hill and out of sight. They disappeared down the brown landscape toward shimmering gray mountains beneath a blue sky.

After Great Pain

After great pain, a formal feeling comes

She was crying when the doorbell rang. It made no difference. It was never convenient. She was always crying now. She had made a cup of tea because at that time of afternoon they always made a cup of tea and sat on the chairs beside the window or out on the balcony with their feet upon the railing, backs to the house, looking gently out, gently talking, telling jokes, laughing as Tel Aviv tarnished from silver to pewter to night.

Now it was always dark before she gathered herself from crying, touched the surprisingly cold tea to her lips and then set the cold cup down. Gone. He had kissed her and walked quickly out the door lugging his gear with his sergeant to help him. And then he drove away as he did every year. And then he was gone. For a left turn into traffic. It wasn't his fault that he was dead. But he was dead. And she was alone with no one to care for, with cold tea in a dark apartment and night coming on.

The photographs on the wall struck no memories, gave no pain. She was the plain girl beside him, unobtrusive at Cannes, incognito at the Berlin festival. Tables of laughing, silly people in Rome, New York, LA. Bright, buoyant, happy faces. Film people. Gorgeous people. And her.

No--not the photographs. The real things hurt her. The red wooden fox, walking on straight legs with black socks and a red tongue sticking out that they bought on location in North Carolina. The dawn-pink acrylic triptych of the desert acid-etched in amber they found in Perpignon. Aztec calendar. Byzantine blown glass. The generous gifts of friends and artists who loved his work and gave to him as he gave to them: freely, with an eye that matched the spirit with the beautiful, and generously--as if he were an eternal spring, a source of infinite plenitude, silvered with sky, and sweet beyond desire.

But now he lay buried in the military cemetery at Kiriat Shaul on a dusty hill where the wind blew, and she was buried in a museum of memories. She had come to hate the real things. She remembered every giver giving and his delight in receiving. Such happy, happy times. They made her cry.

She tried to smile, to be happy with the friends they had gone to school with, served in the army with, worked with, loved. But she couldn't smile and she couldn't eat. Her friends said she was thin. They invited her to Diezengoff for cake and coffee. She went because she didn't have the strength to say "No."

"Life goes on, Aviva," they said. "Come back to work."

She ordered cake, but she couldn't eat it. The coffee didn't clear something in her throat.

"It's been almost a year, Aviva," they said. "You have your own life to lead."

One corner of her mouth turned up at the thought of where her life led.

"The lab's not the same without you," they said. "Everyone in Diagnostics is weeping. Even the Roentgen misses you."

But the slant of light through the trees was too sad. And then, against all reason, she was suddenly charged with joy by the shape of that man there! just disappearing around the ....

And his voice was in her ear. Close. Almost in her mind.

"Arad," it said. "Arad."

It was unmistakably his voice. Sometimes in the night, he would speak to her from across the room.

"Arad," he would say.

Suddenly alert, Aviva sat up, but the room was empty. And dark.

"Arad."

What was so special about a small town in the desert at the end of a road on the way to nowhere? Before the school *bar mitzvah* on Masada twenty years ago, the class had stayed overnight in Arad. They were already friends. He was stationed near there during training, and she had come to visit him on weekends from Sorroca Hospital.

The doorbell rang again, and she rose to answer, turning on lights as she walked toward the door.

A man stood in the shadows of the dark hall. She pressed the button to light the hall. He was a medium man, neither large nor small, her age.

"Would you like to buy an original oil painting?" he said, holding up a large black cardboard portfolio.

The last thing in the world she wanted was art.

But some suggestion of a curve caressed her memory. The shadow at the corner of his mouth tugged at her, a black silk suture in her spirit that hadn't healed.

And then she was suddenly confused by courtesy. She turned away from the door. Let him decide.

"I think you'll really like these," he said following her into the room, starting his pitch, "but I'll let the images speak for themselves."

He set his portfolio on the floor tilted against the coffee table and slipped the knot at the top. The cover fell silently as he opened the flaps. Landscape paintings. He turned them over slowly, overlapping them, as if he were a rug merchant.

"I believe we all exist in Nature and so we can find ourselves in Nature. The purity, the natural grace of every human being, every living thing, finds its image and its fulfillment, its spiritual completion, in the natural world. The beauty of Nature is infinitely echoic of the beauty that is in our souls. And I try in my images to provide the natural window that will allow any perceiver to find himself--or herself--first reflected on the window and at the same time superimposed upon the landscape beyond."

But no nature echoed her beauty. Since he turned left into traffic and abandoned her, she was bereft of loveliness. He had made her feel beautiful. Now no place in the world was plain or barren enough to reflect the aridity of her spirit.

Then, suddenly, she stopped his chatter and the fall of landscape at a speckled one.

"I call this 'Rocky Hillside in the Galil,'" he said.

She stared at the colored fabric through a film of rising tears.

"Look beneath the surface," he said. "Project yourself upon the text and texture of the painting. Some people see an old man, or a woman carrying a burden on her back--a bundle of sticks, maybe. Some see a couple kissing or a face, like the Man in the Moon. You have to open yourself to what's there."

What she saw in the accidental configuration of rocks on a hillside in the Galil was the angle of his smile, happy as he was on the best day of his life.

She sat before the painting, plundered.

And then the artist was beside her on the hassock, his arms around her as she lay her ravaged face gently upon his collar, gently in the comforting hollow of his neck, protected by his shoulder, warmed by his breast. His hand slipped upon her back, stroking her, warming her against the chill.

"I'm sorry, lady." His hand was upon her hair.

"It's all right," she said, resting there cocooned in his ephemeral masculine warmth, finally lifting up from her exotic ruination.

"It's all right," she said, passing a shredded kleenex beneath her eyes.

His shirt-front was stained with her rorschach of tears.

"Do you want me to go?"

"Yes."

He stooped to shuffle his work together.

"Leave that one," she said.

He folded the portfolio, tied the ribbon at the top.

"Come tomorrow at five," she said.

He stood with his portfolio and walked to the door.

"For tea."

2.

The Nerves sit ceremonious, like Tombs--
The stiff Heart questions

They sat on the balcony gently talking, in the aluminum shine of a Tel Aviv afternoon.

"What do you do for a living?" she asked.

"I'm a painter."

"House?"

"No," he said. "I'm an artist. It's my life, my fulfillment in Nature."

"You actually make a living selling paintings door-to-door?" she smiled incredulously. "How much am I going to have to pay for the painting I just bought?"

"Ha-ha," he laughed. "No. Like most people, I have two lives."

"What's your other life?" she asked. "What do you do when you're not an artist?"

"I'm a painter," he said.

"House?" she laughed.

"Ha-ha."

They smiled at each other.

"I'm an interior designer. I'm not very proud of it. I think of it as my dark side. The suppression of my spiritual self, the abnegation of who I am."

She looked at him.

"Have you seen the Sci-Tex building in Haifa?" he continued.

She smiled and shook her hair.

"Or the offices of Elscint Magnetic Resonance Imaging in Tel Aviv?"

She smiled in silent disappointment.

"Three-D Graphic Imaging? That one was written up in *Decorative Arts Today*."

"You must be a famous man."

"Artist," he said. "*Trompe l'oeil* is my specialty."

"So why do you sell paintings door-to-door?"

"Because there's a difference between money and life. I find no resolution in the harmonics of my spiritual vibrations by designing corporate offices. But," he said, gleaming toward her, "my essence staggers in oscillating harmony with the earth. Only when my energy is synchronic with the energy of Nature, saturated with the vitality of the land does my potency achieve totality, my essence consummate in solidarity with the wholeness of Nature."

She looked at him, fascinated by his ability to embrace the commercial and the aesthetic, the mundane and the beautiful.

"Painting is what you do to eat," she said. "Art is what you do to live."

Her simplification startled him. He attributed it to her paramedical training in the army or her homeliness. He felt he was often misunderstood by those whose spirit was untouched by beauty.

Intent upon serving him, she lifted the tea-cozy, hand-woven in Penland, from the pot with the honey Temmoku glaze, and, smiling, she poured him another cup.

3.

The Feet, mechanical, go round--
Of Ground, or Air, or Ought--
A Wooden way
Regardless grown

He lived on George Eliot Street in Tel Aviv in an old building made new by repointed masonry and aluminum windows. His apartment echoed the desert elsewhere. A blue-green cairn from Eilat. Chalk-stone from Rosh HaNikra. Rainbow sand from Moab. The black mud of Ein Gedi. No curtains, no doors anywhere. Free-hanging, split bamboo stalks screened the opening to the bathroom. He slept in a bedroll on the floor of an empty room.

Sometimes, in the blue-white light of very early morning, she would rise from the bedroll and walk the cool tiles through the apartment. In the center of emptiness, she folded her legs within her billowing nightgown and sat down upon a cushion to watch the fragments of elsewhere change color and shape as the silent light came up around her upon a fan of fluted reeds from where the Jordan entered the Kinneret, upon grass and growth, puffs of seed and shucks of plant. An eagle feather.

"My spirit animal," he said.

His office at the other end of the street was at the opposite end of the world from where he lived. She thought of him as a rainbow that arced from one end of George Eliot Street to the other, bridging both the bare natural and the busy mundane. His command of areas she thought mutually exclusive made him appear to alternate between two people at the same time, now a fascinating businessman, now an exciting artist.

His secretary, Shlomit, reflected in the mirrored surface of the desk in the foyer, sat before a glass wall that opened on to a corridor where windows let in sunlight and sky. Rain or shine, the sunlight invariably fell through the window behind her.

Through an archway to the left of the foyer four draftsmen, Varda and Yonatan, sat at tables beside a wall of mirror angled slightly. The door to the right of the secretary opened on a modern office in black and white where the geometry of shape and the absence of accent evoked a moon-lit moon-scape, erratically beautiful and starkly barren.

The one curious photograph in the office held an image of him as a young man standing among mirrors. Two of him were looking out from the left and right of the photograph while between him reflected in mirror were two views of his profile seen from behind his left ear and his right ear. She looked and looked at the picture.

"How did you do this?" she asked.

"What?" He looked up from the architectural sketches he had spread on his desk.

"This photograph."

"Oh," he said, dismissing the obvious, "nothing in Nature is what it is. It's always something else."

Then she noticed the tee-shirts. One said "I'm Smart"; the other said "I'm Smarter."

"How did you do this?" She was genuinely amazed. "Double exposure? Did you graft separate negatives?"

He swiveled the chair and looked at her.

"That's my brother," he said.

"You have a twin brother?"

"Yes. He left the country to find wealth and happiness in the United States. The streets are paved with gold there, in case you haven't heard. The Americans are giving away money."

"I didn't know you had a twin brother. Why have you never mentioned him?"

"He thinks that money is the root of all happiness. He drives a Cadillac. He's a miserable human being. We never seem to agree."

He stood up and came over to her.

"But you and I know that happiness is to be found in the sea."

He put his hand on the back of her neck, beneath her hair, behind her collar.

"And the stars," he said. "And the sky."

She looked up at him as he bent to kiss her. He kept bending, arcing over her. She slipped down upon the couch.

"Here?" She glanced apprehensively at the door.

"Everywhere," he said.

And then, fearful of discovery, she abandoned her body to his body.

4.

A Quartz contentment, like a stone

They left Tel Aviv most Thursday afternoons, wiggling through the sticky, gritty town, spilling out on to the four-lane highways. Landscape lay at the end of every road. He was full of chatter about where he had been and what he had painted. He was always searching elsewhere, and anywhere he stopped was delighting.

The Volkswagen hatch-back, filthy with paint, awkward with easels and taut canvasses, canted over on its right haunch on the rocky hillside. He stepped down from the car and looked around, his eyes already elsewhere, responsive to the gaudy blazoning of light and the thrust of color, his mind already set on the configurations of shape and form, shade and color, force and motion, that lay scattered like a chromatic wash on the surface of the world about him. With wandering steps and slow, he turned about and found a place. He stood and looked, testing the feel of the light.

In the platinum mornings he faced north toward a rhododendron grove in a cleft among arid hills through which the swift Jordan fled to the Kinneret. In the early afternoon, he faced east toward the washed amethystine hills of Jordan as the white sun slacked overhead and then slanted westward, periwinkle blue. Late in the afternoon, he faced south to catch the sea filling with shadows, the scarp of cliff, the dizzying sweep of scatterbrain sky, the touch of blue-gray afternoon on the sides of the basin, amaranthine and mauve to the east, gray-violet to the west.

She became adept at choosing and building the camp by herself, gathering rocks for the fire. She became adroit at breaking the camp by herself, silently collapsing and folding the tent, the bedroll, scouring the dishes with grit from the stream bed so that the metal plates gleamed, killing the fire, packing the car.

She spent those happy days walking, sitting, reading, watching him as he painted. He had a two-hour window of consistent light before he had to change direction. She watched the light. And the world came alive, each day more alive. She sat in shadows and watched the stream, silvered with sky, flashing as the sun turned above it. And then she gathered fallen wood for the fire on which she heated the vegetarian meals she had prepared beforehand.

"I don't think the spirit of any lovely living creature should be extinguished," he said, "so that I can live."

She knew she was there because he needed her. She was content to care for him, because she needed to define herself by serving him. She was who she was in terms of him. She was serene in this new servitude--and yet aware, if only on the lonely nights when she didn't see him, of the wring of loss loosening to the worm of need.

"This is all I ever want," he said in a characteristic moment of intimacy, "to meld my leaping soul with my animist spirit and focus all my creative energies upon the beauty of Nature."

She felt his warm body beside her. Her eyes were on the scintillant sky, and her ears were alert to the hum of the savory night breeze, the murmur of his voice. She felt his naked skin warm upon her naked skin and silky as he anchored his hook in her flesh, a haven for his need.

She thought he meant her.

5.

This is the Hour of Lead--
Remembered, if outlived,
As Freezing persons, recollect the Snow--

"I don't understand," she said. They sat on the porch in the iron evening. The sky was scarred with flecks of rust curling around clouds as the sun set.

"What's there to understand?"

"Why abandon half of your life?"

"Ahh," he said. "I'm not. I'm reaffirming control over all of my life. By abandoning the grubby grasping after money, I'm turning my spirit free to pursue the beautiful all the time. I don't want to spend my time just so that executives with more money than brains can say, 'This office was designed by Tomer Nesher. Interesting, isn't it?' I hate commercialism and the praise of Philistines. I'm not my brother. I won't do it anymore."

She set the table for two. Woven placemats and sterling. When she brought the food to the table and poured the soup, she called him from his book.

"What will happen to Yonatan and Varda?" she asked over the salad.

"The brethren of my spirit will always find a home."

"And Shlomit?"

"Secretaries too."

He looked at her and smiled. "But you're really not interested in them, are you?"

"What will you do?" she asked.

"I will do as the wind does. I will live as the sky lives."

"I don't see why you want to give up that part of your life that sets you free to be an artist."

"I don't want the money, Aviva. I want to be free all the time. I don't want to be locked in a shop. Nature doesn't live in shops and offices."

She scoured the dishes slowly, patiently, as if using grit from the stream bed. She lined them up carefully in the rack above the sink to drip, to dry. And then, when she had bagged the left-overs and put them into the refrigerator, she carefully took down the dishes and wiped them and stacked them and put them away.

"How will you live?" she said, bringing the coffee.

"I'm an artist," he said. "My calling is the beautiful."

She turned on the fan after her shower. When the mist cleared from the mirror, she looked at her face carefully. She could count at the edge of her eyes the years of her youth she had spent in the sun. She gently spread Arise at the corners of her eyes and mouth. She put on panties and nightgown and lay down beside him.

"But how will you live?" she asked in a whisper.

"'God will provide'," he said, laughing.

She laughed too.

"No, really," she said.

6.

First--Chill

On occasional Fridays when they stayed in the city, he erected his display on the pedestrian mall in Nachlat Binyamin. In the summer, the heat that rose from the hot white sidewalk and beat down from the hot white sky was unmoved by the turgid ebb of the epicures of earrings and buyers of bargains, the ill-dressed, unkempt, and young connoisseurs of crafts.

Aviva stood out of the great heat, beneath the awning that shaded a jewelry store. The shadow of the awning emphasized the bright street open to the sky behind her. She watched the torpid flow of sun-lit pedestrian traffic reflected in the window. She saw the palettes of cheap jewelry and the tables loaded with hand-crafts, pottery, weaving. The artists sat on webbed aluminum folding chairs, some beneath sun-umbrellas, some in straw hats. Unless she stood directly between him and the glass, she could see Tomer in the strip of sunlight reflected in the window, his figure and his empty canvasses spread about him like detached scraps of elsewhere.

His work had become ever more minimalist. What once had been evocative landscapes with arcs of tinted joy and jags of dismay that shattered into desperate pointillist shrubbery had become rigid planes of primary color. His solid skies were monochromic canvasses of creamy white or pale blue or the blue that became the yellow and brown of *sharav*. No wind riffled and no wave broke upon the sea that he saw. Shape without form. Shade without color. Paralyzed force. Gesture without emotion.

Each new painting made her uncomfortable. She could no longer find any possible projection of the reality that she saw in the nature that he painted. She didn't know what to say. She turned away from the street to the street reflected in the jeweler's window.

The jeweler's display of precious stones evoked a landscape. Aquamarine and fiery green opal lay scattered near the window to suggest the sparkling waters of a lake. For the beach and the sandy hill that rose behind them, pink and yellow diamonds shaded into topaz; emeralds and jade suggested the forest; black diamonds and jet traced shadows against ruby hillsides. The amethyst evening sky bloomed above.

But because the bright street behind her was reflected in the window, Aviva could most clearly see what was in the jewelry store through the shadow she cast herself. Her outline upon the window was superimposed both upon the landscape within and the reflected streetscape behind her.

The window facilitated the world. Multiple realities, reflected and seen through. Tomer in the bright street, her shadow on the surface of the window, co-mingled with the cold, precious landscape of the jeweler's display.

But where in the window was she, the perceiver perceiving? The shadow projected between being and existence? The cutout through which opposing realities, mutually exclusive, intermingled and meshed?

The miscegenation of reality.

The misogyny of perception.

7.

then Stupor--

"*Trompe l'oeil* is my specialty."

"Don't look at the surface."

"Look beneath the surface."

"I try in my images to provide the natural window that will allow any perceiver to find himself first reflected on the window and at the same time superimposed upon the landscape beyond."

"You have to open yourself to what's there."

"Since we all exist in Nature, we can only find ourselves in Nature."

"The purity, the natural grace of every human being, every

living thing, finds its image and its fulfillment, its spiritual completion, in the natural world."

"Project yourself upon the text and texture of the painted image."

"The beauty of Nature is infinitely echoic of the beauty that is in our souls."

"My essence oscillates in harmony with the earth."

"My potency achieves totality and consummates in solidarity with the wholeness of Nature when my energy is synchronic with the energy of Nature, saturated with the vitality of the land."

"I find no resolution in the harmonics of my spiritual vibrations by dissociating myself from Nature."

"I hate commercialism and the praise of Philistines."

"I've turned my spirit free to pursue the beautiful."

"I want to expand the personal into the universal, to let people see the enormous soul of Nature, to bring the sky into the eyes, the heart, the very being of everything that lives."

"I'm an artist, a painter."

"I am devoted to art, to capturing the effervescent essence for everyone so that we can discover ourselves in Nature and through Nature."

"It's my life, my fulfillment in Nature."

"I don't think the spirit of any lovely living creature should be extinguished so that I can live."

"*Trompe l'oeil* is my specialty."

8.

> *then the letting go--*
> --Emily Dickinson

First she sold the memories. Cherished though they were and aglow with reverence, they were relics from a world she no longer inhabited. Like the seashells and polished stones gathered on the distant shores of her childhood, she disposed of them irrevocably.

She was surprised to discover they were easy to abandon. The Islamic Museum bought the Aztec calendar to rebuild the collection of historic timepieces stolen a decade earlier and never recovered. The Israel Museum bought the Byzantine glass, the sculpture and terra-cotta masks. The place was emptying. She was moving out.

She was simplifying her life by removing all icons of the man she couldn't save with love or care. She emptied the shrine because echoes, like reflections or pain, skewed her perception of the real. Her tears, long dry now, nurtured no memory, reiterated no loss. The man who once stood before her constant vision--as rampant, bloody, and red as an enraged nerve--had deliquesced quietly beneath a dusty military hillside at Kiriat Shaul.

Memory had not tarnished him. He existed without attachment to the things he had touched. Occasionally his name appeared on the screen as Director of Photography on a film the whole country loved.

"Oh, yes," she smiled, remembering.

Otherwise, he was always now at the place where he had stepped out of frame, carelessly waving goodbye from the front door, his sergeant before him. Sometimes, as she went toward the door, she walked through the memory and smiled. As soon as the movers came, he would be gone from there, too.

She didn't despair at diminishing memory because there was another life to save.

"What's going on?" Tomer asked.

"I'm selling things," she said.

Tomer looked around the depleted apartment, the buff walls almost as uniformly brown as some of his minimalist desert paintings.

"What's the price of beauty these days?"

"Depends on what it is and who's buying," she said. "My silver service sold for three times what it cost."

"I don't think it's ever good to sell beauty for money."

"I'm not selling beauty," she laughed, "I'm selling things I don't need, and what I can't sell, I'm giving away."

He inserted his arms beneath the fire-engine red fox and lifted the carved wooden totem.

"You call this beautiful fellow a 'thing'?"

"Things I don't want," she said.

"How can you not want this lovely boy?" He held the fox out at admiring arm's length, drew it up to his face, and kissed it on the lolling, red, wooden tongue.

"He's yours," she said.

He slung the fox beneath his arm as though it were a cat, and looked around the barren apartment.

"You're doing this for me," he said. "I don't need your money."

"No," she said, "I'm doing it for me. I'm moving out."

He stood up straight, stiff, formal as the fox.

"You can't move in with me."

"I know."

"I'm devoted to the beautiful," he said. "I can only be surrounded by the beautiful."

"Yes."

"My art takes precedence over everything else in my life. You know that. You, of all people, know that."

"I don't want to move in with you."

"Oh," he said. "Then where are you going to live," he asked, suddenly concerned for her.

"I'm moving south. Yeroham. Dimona."

"What are you going to do there?"

"I'm a trained nurse. There is always work for a nurse. And nobody wants to go to the south. I can be useful in the desert."

"I can use you right here in Tel Aviv."

"I know," she said.

He walked around the almost bare living room looking at the detritus of her life.

"Are you going to take that with you?" He pointed at the last painting left on the wall. 'Rocky Hillside in the Galil.'

She hesitated for a moment.

"Oh, sure," she said. "Why not."

"A wonderful memory of a happy year spent in the context of the beautiful."

She was amused.

"Whatever," she said.

At the end of the very last road in Arad, beyond the hotels for tourists, a path leads to a monument and then on to a barren promontory that looks out over nothing. The rounded hillside drops sharply away to cold, precious desert for forty kilometers in many directions, a moon-scape as far as the eye can see, the heart can imagine.

Aviva, alone, sat on the tip of nowhere while the world turned amethyst around her. And silver. And gentle. The warm wind kissed her face, caressed her skin, lured the smell of the hospice from her clothing. Lit by the moon, the desert was achingly beautiful, a source of infinite plenitude, silvered with sky and sweet beyond desire. She sat in the center of a lavender world immensely rich in peace and dissolving color. She felt her heart drum, her breath ease, the gravel beneath her hip.

She looked to the sky, and there she was, more white than white, the Figure in the Moon.

Alive! She was alive!

Another Life

"Who's this?" said Stella settling gracefully on the sofa beside him.

"Who's who?" Frank asked. Plucked suddenly from his book, he refocused on the parcel afloat in the silk swirls of her lap.

"These pictures," she said. "And there's a letter with them. 'My darling Stella' . . ."

"Sounds promising," he smiled while his photogray lenses adjusted.

"'My darling Stella,'" she repeated. "'Since I've been here, I've thought of nothing but bright colors--iridescent fish, bougainvillea and frangipani that leap scarlet from the trees, and parraquitoes flashing golden green. The very air is alive with the cries of monkeys, tree-frogs, birds. Sometimes flowers lift away from the vines and become butterflies as big as your hand. Toward evening, I slip naked into the lagoon--and think of you.'"

"Nobody writes like that anymore," said Frank. "Who's it from?"

"See for yourself."

She tipped the package into his lap and drowned his book in kodacolor memories, which he peered at through the bottom third of his glasses.

Blue-green sea. Pellucid sky. A man on the verandah of an elegant house somewhere in sunland. The sundeck of a white boat with the man in the shadow of an awning, colorful drink in hand. An evening scene: candles and fans, the sunshine man in a soft shirt, open at the collar.

"But ... this looks like ...."

"Yes," she said.

"Me," said Frank.

She turned the package over, threw her hair behind her ears.

"Mailed two weeks ago," she said.

Frank looked for the postmark. "Where's it from?"

"Charleroi, in the Dutch Antilles."

"Stella ...."

"How did you do this?" she said, smiling.

"I didn't."

"When was the last time you were away, Frank?"

"Eight months ago," he said. "Yes, this looks just like the Kazakhstan Trade Fair in January."

"Well, they could have been taken anytime, couldn't they?"

"Stella, I've never been in the Caribbean."

"Are you saying this is not you?"

She held a close-up of Frank, his face checkered by sun filtering through a fiber hat.

"Not me," he said.

"Such a clever boy," she said, kissing him. "So full of surprises. What did you do? Find an old roll of film from before we were married?"

"It's not me."

"Sure it is. Or do you have a twin you've been hiding from me?"

"No."

"It looks exactly like you."

Frank looked carefully at the shadowed man.

"Yes," said Frank.

"How exciting for you, Frank," said Stella. "You have another life."

"But someone else is living it," he said.

* * *

On her way to Mann Auditorium the next morning, Stella dropped him, as usual, at the station for the bus up to Jerusalem. "You're not going to do anything funny, are you?" she said. "What do you mean?"

"Well, like take the bus to the Caribbean," she said, kissing him.

"Nah," he said. "Straight to the depths of darkest Jerusalem." The bus climbed out of the humid coastal plain and wound its way through green mountains toward the sky. He looked at the hillside, stone and tree, where the delicate anemone unfolded in the rugged soil.

Sunlight and shadow fell like flickering memories across the old woman in the seat across the aisle. What life did she live outside this bus? Who did she become in the forests of Europe when the sky was dirty with the smoke of burning hair, burning bone? And who was she before she became well-fed and cleanly dressed on the express bus to Jerusalem?

When he arrived, the city was white with morning. He stepped through the wrought-iron gate in the half-wall of stone two streets from the Central Station and climbed the steps out of the stony garden onto the front porch and then into the shadowed gloom of the entrance hall.

"Good morning, Frank." Mira held up a bouquet of faxes that grew overnight in the smoke-free environment. She was wearing sunglasses which did not quite mask her purple cheek.

He clicked on the calendar for the day before he turned to the in-house network. Both Cleo Jacobson, who handled exports, and Lior Liora, who dealt with imports, preferred to dash him electronic notes unless they were already up and moving about with hardcopy.

The default application underlying the screen saver was his cardfile, because when the phone rang in Jerusalem, it was always for him. And he never knew who it was. He would pick up the receiver to hear outlandish sounds. People he never met and would never know started speaking about Bulgarian garden tools or the

Peruvian market for Israeli computer-driven agricultural fertilizer dispensers and automated sprinkler systems.

"Fwang, this Kaburahe Bujumbura. Invoice received in crusados instead for dollars or yen. What going on?"

"'Allo, Rank? Grammasicanpur to speak. What about to identify FOB small rugs as doormats. No import duty on doormats."

"Dis Urzica Csollany Chorkina who speaking. How family, Frang? When expect new shipment automate plastic float device for ...."

"Prank? Prank? That you? Here is Pozdnyakov Mujtaba."

Sometimes he just searched for a sequence of consonants. He would punch in the sounds and hope he had made the right division between personal and family name. He often had to guess whether the voice was speaking from a culture that provided the last name first. Years ago, when his secretary first announced that "Liora, Lior" had arrived for a job interview, he expected a woman.

He always expected a woman, as if excitement were sex-linked and adventure a series of unexpected encounters. He felt powerful in the presence of women who didn't know him. They gave him power, relinquished it actually, and assumed he would be commanding. Women looked at him, poised to obey.

● ● ●

The apartment was dark, the air slightly stale, when he returned to Tel Aviv. He was disappointed. He walked around turning on lights. He played the answering machine.

"Stell? Anat and I are meeting at Picasso. Hope you can join us."

The second caller thought for a long moment but left no message.

He took his book and sat in the light.

"Hi, Frank," said Stella, striding in, her skirt lap creased like bars. "Been home long?"

She came up to him and hugged him--then suddenly thrust him out to arms' length and wrinkled her nose.

"Are you smoking, Frank?"

"I don't think so. I'm sure I would have noticed."

"Your clothes stink of cigarettes."

"They were smoking in the bus station."

"Did you complain?"

"Actually, I think three grandmothers beat the guy up, but the damage was done."

Stella listened to the answering machine.

"Is that where you were? At Picasso's?"

"Yes," said Stella. "Or Paloma. I never know which name goes with which place. They're so much alike."

"Father and daughter," said Frank.

"Funny, Frank. You're getting funny in your old age," said Stella on her way to the shower.

"Who do you think the second caller could have been?" he called after her.

"Sounded like Charles the king," said her voice in the bedroom, "from the Antilles."

And as they sat in the car the next morning, she said, "Are you growing a beard, Frank?"

"I don't think so."

"Forget to shave?"

He raised his hand to his face, as though adjusting a mask.

"What's all that Bohemian stubble, then?" she said. "Are you jealous of my artists? Are you trying to look like Radu Lupu? You're not the artist-type, Frank."

● ● ●

And the first thing that Cleo Jacobson said when she walked into his office was, "Are you in mourning, Frank?"

"No. Why do you ask?"

"Something's the matter with your face. You look like you haven't shaved for a week. Well, look," she said, turning to business, "who do we have in Kuala Lampur to do the customs work on Kibbutz Mayan Zwi's shipment of acrylic lenses?"

That was the business. He was constantly required to be in a country where he had never been, to discover the names and phone numbers of those he didn't know in order to ask them to do a job in a language he did not speak. People obeyed his voice in fact or fax half-way around the world in sunshine or in sorrow. That, too, was power--and complicated because the person who spoke from a hilltop near the bus station in Jerusalem was different from the person imagined by those who heard his voice in Wellington or Trinkamalee. Sometimes he saw himself as the Spider King.

"I know what it is," said Cleo.

"What?"

"You have trifocals."

* * *

Again he was surprised by the darkened apartment in Tel Aviv. The lights on the answering machine glowed at him, unnaturally red and green. He fixed a drink and picked up his book when the phone rang. But the phone in Tel Aviv was never for him. Perhaps it was a call from Charleroi.

"Hello?"

"Oh, hello? Frank? Is that you? Hi. It's Anat. Is Stella there?"

"No, she's not back yet."

"When she comes in would you tell her I called? It's really important. I have so much to tell her, and I haven't seen her for days."

"Didn't you see her yesterday at Picasso?"

"You mean Paloma? No, she didn't show. I think she has a lover, ha-ha."

"Ha-ha," said Frank.

Stella arrived neatly tucked and combed and attentive after

sitting in hot traffic for an hour.

"I like your beard, Frank," she said, sitting beside him and crossing her legs so she could look at him and run her hands over his face. "Did you pencil it in?"

"Just grew," he said.

"So quickly? What did you use? Scott's Lawn Fertilizer?"

"Life in the Caribbean," he said. "All those fecund trade winds contribute to luxurious growth."

"Makes you look sly and French and fifteenth century. It's really quite attractive. The new you?"

"Anat called. She says you have a lover."

"I have sixty-five lovers, all primadonnas of various sexes and ages, not counting the visiting artists, conductors, and soloists. You can have your pick of any or all of them."

"Any one from the Dutch Antilles?"

"You're my only lover in the Caribbean."

"That's the difference between you and me," he said.

"What?"

"All my changes are on the outside."

● ● ●

Lior called out to him from his office as Frank walked past the next morning.

"Frank! I don't know what to do with this currency conversion. There's no market in crusados."

Frank looked at the problem and solved it so elegantly that Lior tilted back in his chair, smiling, and said, "Wow! The George Soros of Jerusalem!"

"Nothing that experience and imagination can't solve," he said.

"What's that on your neck, Frank?"

"What?"

"Looks like a tattoo."

"Ha-ha," they both laughed.

Later in the day as he washed his hands, Frank noticed the greenish stain on the side of his neck. He pulled aside the soft collar of his shirt. It was a new leaf, faintly outlined and pale green.

At the end of a tendril.

Attached to a twisted rope of vine.

Richly colored in blue and green and brown.

That sprang luxuriantly from beneath his belt.

And curled around his breast.

Where a butterfly as big as a hand seemed to lift away.

* * *

The white sun drifted westward to the sea in dramatic orange and purple as he came into the apartment.

"Hi, Frank," she called from the kitchen. "Is that you?"

"And then some," he said.

"I almost didn't recognize you when you came in, Frank, but I'll tell you, I'm getting used to it--I mean, the way it looks, not the way it tickles. Handsome, Frank. You're a handsome man."

"I didn't recognize you in the apron. Are you making dinner?"

"Don't act so surprised. It's not the first time."

"Stella ...."

"Ohh," she said, "are those flowers for me? Frank, how nice. Shall I cook them?"

"Stella. Something's changed."

"Ahh. Guilty flowers. I will cook them," she said, taking a knife from the drawer and neatly cutting off the stem-ends at an angle.

"Not changed, really. More 'happened.'"

"So what happened?"

"I don't think you're going to like it."

"I like the beard."

"This is more radical. Will you put the knife down please?"

"That serious? So what have you done now, Frank?"

"I didn't do anything. It was done to me."

"By whom?"

"I don't know."

"Do you have a lover?"

"No! Do you?"

"You can tell me," she said.

"It's not that."

"What is it, then? Come on. You can be frank with me."

But he didn't laugh. He stood before her, stained with secrets, his image distorted in the curve of her eyes.

Find

He read the letter again. It was clearly a dream, a fiction. When she first brought it into his office, his pallid secretary--who moonlighted as a belly dancer for oriental weddings--held the envelope up to the light, looked at it front and back, laid it carefully before him, and said, "I thought you already paid your debt to society, Sol."

"I certainly did," said Solomon, looking up from the column of figures on the screen. "Two hours every Wednesday night for a month. Why?"

"Looks like the police are after you again. You're a regular law-breaker, aren't you? Are you sure you haven't run another stop sign?"

He read the letter again at the end of the day, when the office had emptied and his partners had left him a legacy of silence. Each time, it said exactly the same thing.

Mr. Solomon Schophet
Malachi Insurance
Tel Aviv

Dear Mr. Schophet:

With regard to Police Report No. 727634/Bet, the items which you deposited with the Lost and Found Division of the City of Tel Aviv have not been claimed. All efforts by the police to discover the owner(s) have not been successful. Pursuant to city ordinance, this item reverts to the possession of the finder. Would you please, at your earliest convenience, retrieve the item, designated lot No. 727634/Bet, from the Lost and Found Division at City Hall.

Yours truly.

So what does one do with a black velvet wallet containing five unset diamonds roughly estimated at a quarter of a million dollars? Solomon had reported the find within an hour of having come upon the wallet in the street. Since he expected the person who had lost them to claim them, he forgot about them, his imagination having long since ceased to frolic with the idea of possessing them. He told Revital about finding them and turning them in to the police, but all she would say was, "Where did you find a place to park around City Hall?" What was she going to say now?

The elevator door opened upon a dark hall. In the light spilling from the elevator, he found the right button to light the hall, and in the light from the hall he found the right key to open the door.

He walked into a silent house. He could have been a gang of riotous thieves come to ransack the apartment, roll up and carry away the delicately worn rose-colored Persian carpet, snatch from the china cabinet the crystal wedding presents unused for thirty years, and bag the silver candle sticks from the dining table. He would have been a disappointed gang of riotous thieves because there was nothing else to steal.

He hung his suitcoat in the hall closet and set his briefcase beside his chair in the living room. He stood outside the bedroom door. He heard the squeak of the keyboard. He tapped lightly and entered.

"Oh!" she startled. "Solly. Is it six-thirty already? My God, how the day flies! Just a minute, let me save." She looked at the screen and said, "F-5."

His bedroom had become a shocking place. When her first book, written with the old green-gray Olympia manual on the kitchen table, won the Writer's Union prize as the best first novel by an Israeli author, they had a carpenter build her a desk from the window to the corner and from the corner to the door. Her desk was littered with open books, stacked books, dictionaries, and volumes of the encyclopedia all bristling with slips of paper; the foot of the bed was covered with galley-proof in various states of correction, the floor around the bed was awash in sheets of paper.

While her machine whirred to save, she stood up and put her loving arms around his shoulders and kissed him and said, "What's rollicking in the insurance business today? Did you settle lots of claims and make lots of people happy?"

"Oh, the usual," he said. "Loss and theft. Orphans and widows. Found two hundred and fifty thousand dollars."

"Really? That's unusual. How careless of you to misplace them."

"Yes," he said. "We get to keep those diamonds I found last year."

"Wonderful. I really need some paper clips and wondered where the money was going to come from."

"I'd be glad to get you a box of paper clips if that would make you happy."

"Very happy. You know, the big ones." She kissed him.

"Mmmm. That's all it takes?" He kissed her.

"Listen. If I have a box of paper clips, just think of all the things I can put together."

"Chapter One? Chapter Four? Dinner?"

"Right," she laughed. "I can even put together dinner. Seven-thirty? That gives me another half-an-hour to work."

"What's happening?"

"Haim has withdrawn sexually and emotionally from Dora. Dora suspects he has another woman, but he actually has been diagnosed HIV positive."

"That's pretty rare here, isn't it? There are only one-hundred-and-thirty-five cases in the whole country."

"The unexpected is what makes it surprising. Her moral question is whether to confront him with the suspected infidelity and risk losing him; and his moral question is whether to reveal to the woman he mostly loves that the very act of loving her will destroy her."

"Ah, the moral question."

"Always," she said.

"Seven-thirty is fine."

He sat in the living room, but didn't open his briefcase. Tiny curls of pale steam rose from his cup of tea. He opened Sandbank's translation of Chaucer, but he didn't read.

There would be no question if the children needed money, but Roi was comfortably married in the north. Roi saw his life in terms of service to the kibbutz and to the country; he had everything that he needed and was philosophically opposed to having anything more or better than anyone else on the kibbutz. And Ayalla was philosophically committed to repairing human beings imperfect in the area between the neck and the abdomen. Her idea of new clothes was a fresh lime-green surgical gown which Rothschild Hospital generously provided. He was always amused to think where and how his children absorbed such preposterous values.

And them? Revital's books were selling, being reprinted, and selling more. Her agent was negotiating a movie contract for the third novel. She didn't need more money or more house; she needed more hours in the day. And he had everything he ever wanted in this life: a happy and productive wife, infinitely fascinating after all these years, and children who were happy with lives they designed for themselves.

Seven-thirty came and went as it almost always did. He turned on the lights in the kitchen, set the table. He took from the refrigerator three cucumbers, two tomatoes, an onion, and four eggs. He cut the ends from the cucumbers and the stem-spot from the tomatoes with a paring knife, then diced the cucumbers, tomatoes, and half the onion into a Pyrex bowl which he put on the table with a plastic container of humus. He scrambled the eggs with the other half of the onion, seasoned them with a dash of salt and a twist of the pepper-mill, and spilled them into the olive oil sizzling in the frying pan. He cut and toasted the rolls, poured the cold water which they kept in a green prune-juice bottle in the refrigerator, and set the chipped kettle on a low fire for coffee afterwards.

Then he tapped on the bedroom door.

"Dinner's ready," he said.

"What? You're kidding!" Revital looked at her watch. "I'm sorry, but I'm just not in this world. Mmmm, smells wonderful. Thank you. F-5," she said, peering at the screen.

"The hardest thing about fiction," she said as they sat at the little table in the kitchen, "is not the fiction but the truth."

"So what's going to happen?"

"Well, I know what I would do, but I don't know what Haim would do. What's true for me wouldn't necessarily be true for him. Men are a mystery."

"And Dora?"

"Oh," she said, "Dora will confront him. She has enough sense of self to realize that she will continue to be who she is even without the man she feels has lied to her. The relationship is good for her only so long as it is truthful. When their relationship shifts to deception and half-truths--already signaled by Haim's withdrawal--then all obligations are dissolved. What moral obligation does one owe to a relationship one no longer wants?"

"But she only thinks the relationship is built on half-truths," Solomon said. "Actually it's not. Haim has a disease, after all, not a mistress."

"The half-truth is not what he has or how he got it--that, don't you see, is the truth. The half-truth is what he hasn't told her and that he hasn't told her. And because he hasn't told her, she thinks he has a mistress."

"Does thinking make it so?" Solomon was skeptical.

Revital explained again, more slowly: "What she thinks is true ... is true for her ... whether it is true for him ... or true in fact ... or not."

Solomon laughed. "So truth is relative," he said, "depending on who sees it and how they see it."

"Yes," she said.

"Sounds like fiction to me," he said.

"Pre-cise-ly," she said.

Solomon smiled at Revital's equation. "But that doesn't help Haim, does it? Haim should open his eyes and see the truth. Maybe," said Solomon, "he could find some diamonds."

"Don't be silly. That sort of thing doesn't happen in the real world."

"But they're worth a lot of money," Solomon said. "I even know where he could find them."

"The money is useless, don't you see? It won't cure his AIDS."

"He could go on a spree," said Solomon.

"He may be a man, but he's not a child."

"An intellectual spree, then," Solomon revised.

"Yes. Okay," Revital conceded. "But he doesn't need money for that. And it doesn't solve the moral problem, does it? Money's irrelevant. It's like someone giving him a ... a..." she searched for the most useless thing she could think of. "A motorcycle," she said at last.

"Speaking of someone giving you a motorcycle, what do you think I should do with the diamonds?"

Taking cup and saucer in hand, she rose to return to her work. "Don't spend all the money in one place," she said, "and call me when the news is on."

2.

"I'm so mad at you," she said the next morning at breakfast. Though she only went as far as the bedroom, she was already dressed for work in an elegant white silk blouse and incongruous pink sweat pants.

"Why? What have I done now?"

"You were in my dreams again."

"I'm not responsible ...."

"Yes, you are. It's your fault."

"What did I do this time?"

"Well, I was dreaming about Dora and Haim."

"How did I know you were dreaming about Dora and Haim?" he said.

"My subconscious was working out Haim's moral problem--the relationship between telling the truth and causing pain--and it was a splendid scene. Dora and Haim had stopped their car in the Ramat Gan Safari Park. They were together and alone, protected by the car from the dangerous animals in the world outside, and yet their very isolation and intimacy provided a dangerous context for the escape into truth that each was struggling with. It was a lovely scene. You see, the symbolic aspects of the physical situation accurately reflected their emotional states and encapsulated the theme of the novel."

"Yes, very nice," said Solomon.

"When all of a sudden--goddamn it!--there you were striding across the fields! It was definitely you. No doubt about it. In my dream! You came around that little lake, completely oblivious to a tiger lying across your path. The tiger stood up as you approached. I was terrified it was going to jump, but you turned and gave it a beatific smile, you know the way you do, and it just went away. And then, and then--I really couldn't believe your *chutzpah*--you came up to Haim and Dora's car. You chased away the monkeys who were sitting on the hood chewing the windshield wipers with their muscular mouths and sharp teeth. You opened the door and you said, 'Haim, I'm your rich uncle from America. I've come to bequeath you a quarter of a million dollars.'"

"Good idea," said Solomon.

"It's a terrible idea. I was so furious, I woke up. It's a phony sort of contrived event that makes no story believable."

"But it's not a story," Solomon reminded her. "It's a dream and they aren't supposed to be believable."

"Mine are. This was. Haim was about to make a decision. I

was about to find out what it was. And here you come, *deus ex machina*, stumbling into my story and wrecking it, too."

"I'm sorry, dear. More coffee?"

"Now I'll never know what Haim would have done."

"Did he at least thank me for the money?"

"I'm angry at you," she said. "Thank you. A little more milk."

"I thought something was the matter. You were twisting and groaning and making all sorts of animal noises last night. That was about four."

"I was in the Safari Park."

"I didn't think of that. I thought maybe my light was bothering you."

"Oh, didn't you sleep last night?"

"Not very much."

"Of course not. You were too busy wandering about the Safari Park and meddling with my dreams. Serves you right. That'll teach you to keep out of my dreams. I'm serious," she said.

3.

Solomon had to make a decision about the diamonds and the money. Since he neither needed nor wanted the diamonds, the only thing to do was to get rid of them. But he had them. But he didn't want them. But he had them.

Of course, if he did nothing, the problem would evaporate by itself. The wallet would remain among the unclaimed Found items until some clerk stole it or it came up for auction. The money would go to the city. It would be like paying an extra quarter of a million dollars in taxes.

"I've come to collect lot No. 727634/Bet," he said, reading from the letter to the officer at the desk.

"Are you a criminal?"

"Of course not," said Solomon, surprised at the accusation.

"This is where we book criminals," said the officer without smiling. He was tangled in the bitterness of his job. "You want

Lost and Found. Go straight on down the hall and turn right."

"I've come to collect lot No. 727634/Bet," Solomon said, handing the letter to the officer behind the security grate.

The officer returned with a black velvet wallet in a plastic sack. He spilled it out onto the counter.

"This it?"

"Looks like it."

"Better open it to make sure."

He opened it. Five shiny slips of stiff, milky paper, each folded into a packet and slipped into a slot in the wallet; each packet contained a single stone; each stone would ransom a princess from a wizard.

"Ah, the man who found the diamonds."

"Yes. Why didn't anyone claim them?"

"Well," said the officer expansively; he fancied himself a natural philosopher and master of psychology. "Many reasons. A lot of people wouldn't believe that anyone who found them would turn them in. Some people would rather take the loss than come to the police. And some people might not even know that they were missing. They're probably insured anyway."

"Five diamonds? A quarter of a million dollars? Maybe more?"

"Look" said the officer. "It may be big money to you and me, but let's face it, it's not big money to everybody."

They stood, looking at the stones.

"Will you need some police protection until you get these diamonds to your vault?"

"No, I don't think so. Thank you."

"Be careful then. Somebody might jump you."

Solomon dismissed the possibility with a smile. But as he came down the steps of City Hall, people stared at him as though he were a criminal. Kids with pierced faces, wild hair, and tattoos lingered on the square and traced his progress with more than casual interest as though prepared to jump him. He tried to look nonchalant, but he started to perspire. He hailed a cab and drove home protected from the dangerous animals in the world outside.

Once he was safely at home, the problem remained: what to do with the diamonds. Or, put another way, what was his moral obligation to something he didn't want, hadn't asked for? If he wasn't going to give it to the city of Tel Aviv, then who was he going to give it to? The streets were full of urchins who would only use it to buy hats and get tattoos. The poor people in the city were not starving. The Russian and Ethiopian immigrants were being cared for--not to anyone's satisfaction, but five diamonds wouldn't dent that problem. He might improve the quality of life for a dozen families, but only temporarily.

He abandoned the idea of giving the diamonds to fight cancer or diabetes or AIDS. A cure for AIDS might help Haim, but the problem was too big and the value of the diamonds too small to make any real contribution in that direction.

He was not interested in fame. Revital's books already brought them more fame than they could comfortably handle: offers ("Let me help you promote your ...") and invitations ("Speak here," "Speak there") that diminished and circumscribed their lives rather than expanding them. He was not vain. He had no ego invested in his business, and he was content to sell it to strangers when it no longer challenged his intellect.

He slept fitfully. He eliminated what he imagined were all the possibilities in the world. And then one night, as he was reading and nodding between sleep and poetry, he broke bright awake and knew what he had to do. He decided to break the law. He turned over with a smile and went to sleep at the brim of dawn.

4.

"I hope you're not angry at me this morning," he said as she swept into the kitchen, hair wonderfully awry, and took her place at the table.

"Solly, darling, how could I ever be angry at you?"

"Well, sometimes you're unhappy when I appear in your

dreams."

"Of course! You deserve it. You have no business in my dreams. And don't try to pretend you're innocent."

"Try some of that strawberry confiture. It's Rumanian. I found it in the supermarket."

"Umm. Thanks," she said. "Did I tell you I found out what Dora and Haim are going to do? No thanks to you, by the way."

"Did it come out of a dream or what?"

"No, I just sat down and figured it out. An intellectual spree, you might say."

"So?"

"Actually, it was mutually satisfactory. She decided to leave him and he decided to leave her."

"What's satisfactory about that?" Solomon wanted to know.

"She felt she couldn't trust a man she couldn't trust, and he felt he couldn't love a woman he couldn't love--and anyway, he's going to die soon."

"I don't find that very satisfactory at all."

"You mean not very romantic," she corrected.

"All right, not very romantic."

"Or sentimental," she added.

"Or sentimental."

"You keep forgetting," she said, "that this is the real world we're dealing with here--not some sentimentalized version of what we want to happen in the real world. People die. People look out for themselves. Not everyone is as self-contained as you are."

"What sort of moral imperative does that serve?" he asked.

"The moral imperative not to get stuck in intellectual ruts. Not to accept the framework of the given. Not to place limits on reality. Not to let sentimental expectations blind you to the possible."

"You're wonderful," he laughed, and he leaned over the table to kiss her.

"I know," she said. "But excuse me now. I must get these little gems of wisdom into prose."

"Okay. I'll be home by six-thirty. As usual."

"As usual," she echoed. "By the way, speaking of gems. Did you decide what you're going to do with the diamonds?"

"I have."

"Nothing syrupy and sentimental, I hope."

"Nothing that will ever show up in your dreams."

"I hope not," she said, disappearing into the bedroom, closing the door behind her.

Solomon cleared the table, briskly washed the dishes and set them in the rack above the sink to drip and dry. He squeezed the soap from the pink sponge and wiped the crumbs from the table into the palm of his hand and brushed them from his hands into the sink. He ran the water to clear the sink, wiped it down with the sponge, and dried his hands on the dish towel.

He took his suitcoat from the closet, picked up his briefcase and his keys and, just before closing the door on the scene, he gives five diamonds to you. Yes, you. Here they are.